"I want my son back."

Her head hung down and her shoulders shook with the force of silent sobs.

Joe stood helpless in the face of Maggie's despair. When words wouldn't come, he pulled her into his arms and pressed her face against his shoulder. He held her for a long time without speaking.

"It's so cold outside," she whispered, her breath warm against his chest. "They didn't even take his blanket."

Joe swallowed the knot of regret in his throat. "We'll find him."

With Joe's arms around her, Maggie felt as if she'd come home. Hope feathered the inside of her stomach. Even after her tears dried, she didn't lift her head, didn't want to move from the certainty of Joe's embrace. Despite the pain of their past, he was the only man she trusted to find her son alive.

And she'd sell her soul to the devil himself to get Dakota back.

ELLE JAMES

LAKOTA BABY

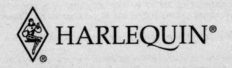

TORONTO • NEW YORK • LONDON
AMSTERDAM • PARIS • SYDNEY • HAMBURG
STOCKHOLM • ATHENS • TOKYO • MILAN • MADRID
PRAGUE • WARSAW • BUDAPEST • AUCKLAND

This book is dedicated to my children—Courtney, Adam
and Megan—and to my grandson—Reily. If ever I lost
one of you, I'd be as frantic as my heroine, Maggie, to get
you back. Children are to be loved and cherished. They
outgrow their parents entirely too fast. I love you guys!

ISBN-13: 978-0-373-22961-1
ISBN-10:   0-373-22961-5

LAKOTA BABY

Copyright © 2006 by Mary Jernigan

This edition published by arrangement with Harlequin Books S.A.

® and TM are trademarks of the publisher. Trademarks indicated with
® are registered in the United States Patent and Trademark Office, the
Canadian Trade Marks Office and in other countries.

www.eHarlequin.com

Printed in U.S.A.

ABOUT THE AUTHOR

Golden Heart winner for Best Paranormal Romance in 2004, Elle James started writing when her sister issued the Y2K challenge to write a romance novel. She managed a full-time job, raised three wonderful children and she and her husband even tried their hands at ranching exotic birds (ostriches, emus and rheas) in the Texas Hill Country. Ask her and she'll tell you what it's like to go toe-to-toe with an angry 350-pound bird! After leaving her successful career in information technology management, Elle is now pursuing her writing full-time. She loves building exciting stories about heroes, heroines, romance and passion. Elle loves to hear from fans. You can contact her at ellejames@earthlink.net or visit her Web site at www.ellejames.com.

Books by Elle James

HARLEQUIN INTRIGUE

906—BENEATH THE TEXAS MOON
938—DAKOTA MELTDOWN
961—LAKOTA BABY

CAST OF CHARACTERS

Joe Lonewolf—Painted Rock Reservation tribal police chief, sworn to carry on the ways of his Lakota ancestors.

Maggie Brandt—Joe's former lover and widow of his dead stepbrother. Will her secret ruin her chances with Joe?

Dakota—Maggie's five-month-old son, kidnapped and ransomed.

Bill Franks—Ex-con turned vending machine delivery man. Is he delivering more than snacks to the residents of the Painted Rock Indian Reservation?

Gray Running Fox—Joe's old friend and manager of the Grand Buffalo Casino.

Tokala—The mysterious drug dealer supplying methamphetamines to the Lakota youth.

Marcus Caldwell—National Indian Gaming Commission representative to the Grand Buffalo Casino.

Randy Biko—The leader of the Sukas gang.

Delaney Toke—Tribal police officer and Joe's right-hand man.

Leotie Jones—A woman obsessed with Joe Lonewolf. Would she do anything to get him?

Chapter One

She stood on a slight rise in the middle of a prairie, the golden grasses wilted and dying. Winter hovered on the horizon, gray clouds growing ever larger, harbingers of the snows to come.

Despite her goose-down jacket, she shivered, wondering where she'd left her gloves and hat. Anyone with sense wouldn't come out in subzero temperatures without the proper clothing. Had she lost her mind?

As she pondered this conundrum, she heard a bleating sound as if a lamb had been separated from its mother. Where did the cry come from? She spun three-hundred-sixty degrees but all she could see was prairie for miles and miles. Not another living soul, animal or human, just herself alone on an endless plain.

Was it an animal separated from its mother? Her heart wept for the frightened creature.

Thinking she might have imagined the sound, she turned to find her way home. Home to the little cottage on Painted Rock, the South Dakota Indian Reservation where she lived with her son, Dakota.

The cry sounded again, only this time less like a lamb and more like the plaintive whimper of a baby.

Her baby.

"Dakota?" Her heartbeat picked up pace until it pounded against her ribcage. She couldn't see her son in the vastness of the open prairie. Why was she here? Why had she left Dakota alone in his bed?

She took off at a run, knowing neither the direction nor the distance to town. All she knew was that she had to get to Dakota. He was crying—he needed her. The more she ran, the slower her legs moved until she slid into a wallow, her legs dragged down by the weight of cold, clammy mud filling her boots and coating her clothes.

"Can't stop. Must get to Dakota." Leaning to the side, she grasped an outstretched branch from a tree she hadn't seen a moment before. The branch became a hand, locking with her fingers, dragging her to safety, freeing her from the pit of glue-like sludge.

For a moment, she lay with her face on the ground, gasping for breath. When she lifted her head to thank her rescuer, her dead husband stared down at her, his face slashed with blood, his eye sockets vacant. Again, he held out his hand to help her to her feet.

Maggie screamed and fell backward into the ditch, the sucking mire like fingers grasping at her arms and legs, dragging her deeper and deeper until mud covered her face, filling her lungs. When she thought her chest would explode from lack of air, blessed blackness swallowed her.

MAGGIE BRANDT sat straight up in bed, shaking.

"Dakota," she said into the darkness, pulling in deep breaths of cool night air.

Her digital clock glowed—4:15 a.m. It wasn't due to go off for another two hours. With her heart still pounding in her ears, she knew she wouldn't get back to sleep.

Had she been startled awake by the dream? Or had Dakota really cried out in his sleep?

Shivering, Maggie slung the covers aside and slid from her bed. She padded barefoot across the carpeted floor, her feet moving more freely than they had when mired in the mud of her nightmare.

Why was it so cold in the house? If it was this chilly in her room, what about the baby's room? Had he kicked his covers off? Why hadn't he woken up crying?

Her steps quickened.

To conserve on her gas bill, she'd set the heat five degrees lower than usual. Had she turned it down too low?

On the way down the hall toward Dakota's room, she passed the thermostat with only a cursory glance, determined to fix the heating problem after she'd assured herself that Dakota was okay. Tendrils of frigid air caressed her bare feet and calves, rising from the floor. Her breath caught in her throat, making it difficult for her to fill her lungs.

Frigid night air drifted in from the bedroom in front of her—it had nothing to do with the thermostat.

"Dakota." Maggie raced into the minuscule room, barely large enough for the baby's furniture. The small window stood wide open, the blue-and-white cloud curtains flapping in the bitter wind.

"Oh my God," Maggie whispered. Her feet carried her one agonizing step at a time toward the crib of her five-month-old son, her heart choking the air from her throat.

Even before she peered through the colorful mobile into the nest of blue blankets, she knew.

Dakota was gone.

A SHRILL BEEPING NOISE pierced his sleep, forcing Joe Lonewolf awake. He fumbled in the dark for his pager, until his fingers curled around it and he lifted it close to his face. In bright green digital letters he read Call Maggie, followed by a phone number and 911.

His pulse raced through his veins and as he swung out of bed the blankets and sheets fell in a careless heap to the floor.

Why would Maggie call at…he peered at his clock…four-twenty in the morning? Hell, why would Maggie call at all?

He grabbed for the phone and dialed the number, every cell in his body on high alert.

"Joe?" Maggie answered the phone before it had barely rang once. "I need you." Her words came out in a sob, reaching across the line like a hand curling around his heart.

"What's wrong, Maggie?" He could hear the faint wail of a siren in the background. "Are you okay?"

No response, only the sound of someone taking a ragged breath.

"Maggie! Talk to me!" he shouted, panic tightening his chest.

"Joe, Dakota's gone." A sharp clattering crackled across the line and the phone went dead.

What the hell was going on? Before he could form another coherent thought, he was throwing on clothes, a jacket and hopping into his boots. He hit the door running. Maggie needed him. He had to get there.

Outside his house, the predawn air hit him like a slap in

the face. What was it, minus ten degrees already? And it wasn't even the end of October. The first snow hadn't fallen.

His black SUV had a thin layer of ice covering the windshield and it took two cranks before the engine turned over. Maggie needed him. The thought replayed through his head, a mantra to keep him moving forward when he could hardly see through the windshield.

Dust and gravel spewed to the sides as he spun the vehicle out of his driveway. He raced down the road until he passed the bright green city limit sign for Buffalo Bluff, the largest town on the Painted Rock Indian Reservation. For once in his life, he wished he didn't live so far out of town. The eight miles to the small community took an eternity. At the same time, the drive gave him too much time to think about Maggie—his stepbrother's widow.

Had it only been two weeks since Paul's accident? It seemed like a month had passed from the time he'd received the call that his stepbrother had run off the road on his way home from work at the Grand Buffalo Casino. He'd been pronounced dead at the scene, leaving behind his wife and baby.

Joe slammed his hand to the steering wheel, still angry he hadn't lived up to the promise he'd made his mother— to watch out for Paul.

Now Paul was dead. But his baby had his whole life ahead and he needed someone to look out for him. What had Maggie meant, he was gone?

Dakota. The baby boy still gnawed at Joe's gut. *He should have been mine.* As soon as the thought surfaced, Joe pushed it down. He had no right to feel that way. *Maggie should have been mine.* His foot left the accelerator and his Explorer slowed in its headlong race across the reservation. None of this was supposed to happen.

Maggie wasn't supposed to marry Paul, Paul wasn't supposed to die, and Dakota should be tucked in bed sleeping like the baby he was. Why then was he racing into town, fear gripping his chest?

Joe skidded his SUV against the curb next to the little house on Red Feather Street and slammed the shift to Park. As he leaped from the vehicle, he squinted at the bright array of lights from squad cars and state police vehicles. The wind had died down during the night, but the smell of snow sifted through the morning air.

He blinked at the glare of headlights and strobes, his eyes stinging in the frosty air. Four hours of sleep wasn't much to go on and he hadn't had a drop of caffeine since yesterday noon. Not that he needed caffeine.

Not since Maggie's call.

Delaney Toke, one of Joe's tribal police officers, stepped down from the concrete porch. "Glad you came. She just sits there, rocking back and forth."

"What happened?"

"Apparently, someone came in during the night and stole the baby."

Although he'd been prepared by Maggie's words, Joe still felt the bottom drop out of his stomach. "How, when?"

"We don't know. All we can guess is somewhere between midnight and four-fifteen this morning when she called."

"Thanks, Del." He moved around the officer and strode toward the door.

Maggie might be his brother's widow, but she'd been Joe's woman first. Until he'd gone to Iraq. He didn't regret the time he'd served for his country, but he did regret the time he'd been away. He'd never thought Maggie would marry Paul.

But why wouldn't she? Joe hadn't made any promises—he'd actually told her they had no future and not to wait for him.

Standing in desert BDUs with his duffel bag slung over his shoulder, he'd fought his desire to take her into his arms as her face paled and her eyes pooled with tears. Had he really expected her to wait around for his return from the dangers of war? He'd been a bastard and gotten what he deserved when he came home to find Maggie married.

Too tired to think or to allow old memories to clutter his head, he sighed and turned toward the door. A state policeman was unrolling yellow crime scene tape around the yard to cordon off Maggie's house from curious neighbors.

A cameraman from the satellite station out at the casino was already panning the scene. Joe bypassed the man and headed for the door.

"Hey, Joe," Del called out. "Sorry about your nephew."

Joe nodded briefly, his gut clenching the closer he got to the door. He hadn't seen Maggie since his stepbrother's funeral. But she'd called him. Fear for her child must have made her desperate. Joe knew she'd rather call anyone but him after how he'd treated her over a year ago.

Brown grass crunched beneath his feet, brittle from the subzero nights. A few tenacious leaves clung to the ash tree in the front yard, soon to be whipped away by forty-mile-an-hour winter winds. He tried to focus on the insignificant details, instead of on his imminent meeting with the woman he'd spent the better part of a year trying to forget.

Had she married Paul out of revenge?

No. Maggie wasn't the vengeful type. Then, had she always been in love with Paul? Joe felt his chest contract. Had their night of passion been nothing but lust, just as he'd told her?

The letter from Leotie two months after his deployment to Iraq said it all. Maggie and Paul had gotten married not long after Joe'd left. She said they were happy, in love and expecting a baby.

The news hit him like a mortar to his belly.

As he'd walked night patrols in the desert, he'd wondered what Maggie would have done if he'd asked her to wait for him. Would she have married Paul anyway?

He'd been certain Maggie had no place on the reservation or in his Indian way of life. Just as he'd made a promise to his mother to watch out for his stepbrother, he'd made another promise to his father to raise his sons to know the Lakota ways. Maggie would not fit in with that promise. She was white, he was Indian. Their two worlds could not converge— or so he'd thought a lifetime ago, before he'd gone to war.

Now he was here for Dakota. The little boy with the face of an angel. With dark auburn hair curling around his head, he was the image of his mother. It hurt Joe to look at him. The child perched in his mother's arms at Paul's funeral, staring with wide, brown eyes at the gathering of people. Oblivious to the seriousness of the occasion, he hadn't understood the finality of his father's death.

Joe told himself the boy was his primary reason for standing in front of the little clapboard house, not his mother.

Maggie appeared in the doorway as if conjured from his deepest thoughts. Her pale skin was almost translucent, the light dusting of freckles even seeming faded. Yet, despite her red-rimmed eyes, she was every bit as beautiful as the first time he'd seen her in the tribal youth center. She'd stood out like a flame amidst the dark-haired, dark-skinned teenagers she was shooting hoops with.

Standing with her hands drooping at her sides, the agony in her gaze pierced Joe's soul in a way he hadn't expected, and his arms ached to hold her and soothe away the fear and anguish.

Then he remembered how quickly she'd gone into another man's bed after he'd left—the bed of his stepbrother he'd resented as a child growing up.

His lips firmed into a straight line and he nodded. "Maggie."

A single tear slid down her cheek. "Dakota's gone." She wrapped her arms around her middle and shivered. Dressed only in jeans and an oversized green sweatshirt, she wasn't up to the cold of the late-October prairie breeze.

Joe had the sudden urge to walk away—no, make that run—as far away as he could get from her. But he couldn't leave Maggie when she was so vulnerable. "Let's go inside." For the better part of the last month, he'd avoided her at every turn—a tough thing to do in such a small community. Especially when he was a tribal policeman and she worked with the reservation youth. Sometimes they crossed paths. He worked hard to make those occasions brief.

She led the way into the living room and waved at the couch, muttering something about sitting. Yet Maggie stood half turned away from him, her gaze on the scene outside the window as if watching for her son's return.

Joe shrugged out of his coat and slung it onto a chair. The two state police officers moved in and out of the house, talking to each other and into the radios they carried. To Joe, Maggie might as well have been the only one in the room.

After one long minute, he couldn't stand the silence any longer. He walked up behind her and pressed a hand to her shoulder. "Maggie, sit. I can't talk to you when you have your back to me."

"I'm sorry. It's just…" Her hand made a weak wave. "I can't focus. I can't think." Then she turned and stared straight into his eyes. "I want my son back. Oh, God, I want him back." Her head hung down and her shoulders shook with the force of silent sobs.

Joe stood helpless in the face of her grief. When words wouldn't come, he pulled her into his arms and pressed her face against his shoulder. He held her for a long time without speaking.

"It's so cold outside," she whispered, her breath warm against his chest. "They didn't even take his blanket." Burrowing against him, her tears soaked into his chambray shirt.

A twinge of jealousy skittered across his consciousness to be squelched in the rightness of a mother's tears for the son she'd lost. The son she'd had with Paul. Joe swallowed the knot of regret in his throat. "We'll find him."

WITH JOE'S ARMS around her, Maggie felt as though she'd come home. Hope feathered the inside of her stomach. Even after her tears dried, she didn't lift her head, didn't want to move from the certainty of Joe's embrace. She knew if she did, the gaping black horror of the past would rush back to overwhelm her.

Joe pressed a finger beneath her chin and tipped her face upward, breaking through her wall of thoughts. "Maggie, what time did you notice Dakota missing?"

The blinking red of her alarm clock pierced her clouded memory. "Four-fifteen. I woke because it was cold in the house. They could have taken him between the time I went to bed around midnight and when I awoke." His touch made her want to lean on him and let him shoulder her burden. But this was Joe.

She jerked her chin out of his grip, hardening the heart she'd given him freely once. If not for the loss of her son, she would have nothing to do with him. But despite the pain of her past, he was the only man she trusted to find her son alive. And she'd sell her soul to the devil himself to get Dakota back.

"Did you hear anything, see anything?"

She'd answered all these questions for Delaney but Joe needed to know as much as he could to search for her son on the reservation. The FBI hadn't arrived yet, but Maggie would bet her son's life on Joe. She inhaled and let the air out slowly, combing through her barely conscious memories of the past hours. "No. I didn't see or hear anything." Her voice caught and she bit hard on her lip to keep from shedding more tears.

She concentrated on Joe and it was as if she could see his thoughts churning in eyes so brown they could be black. His hair had started to grow out from his tour of duty with the South Dakota National Guard. He looked more like the tribal police officer she'd known rather than the unbending military man she'd seen at her husband's funeral.

Officer Toke stepped in the door and nodded toward Joe.

Maggie held her breath hoping for news. Something tangible.

Joe pushed to his feet and strode across the room. "Did you find anything outside?"

The man shook his head. "The ground is hard and dry. Without snow, we couldn't trace footprints."

Maggie leaped to her feet and joined the men. "What about fingerprints?"

The police officer shook his head. "Dusted and sent to the state crime lab. Takes time to identify each. We'll need yours to match up."

She nodded but her shoulders sagged, the heavy burden of her failure pushing them down. "How could they just come in and leave without a trace? I was in the house all the time," she whispered. A shiver rippled down her back.

Joe reached out and pulled her against him. "It's not your fault, Maggie."

"But I should have woken up."

His fingers tightened on her forearms. "We'll find him."

She stared up into his dark, swarthy face, his high cheekbones and strong chin, evidence of his power and ancestry. He was Lakota, one of the surviving members of a proud nation of Sioux warriors. If anyone could find her son, he could.

The aching emptiness in her belly eased, followed quickly by an acidic froth of guilt. She should have told him her secret when she'd found out about it, before he left for the Middle East. But the time had passed. Now she had to keep the knowledge to herself.

Tribal police officer Delany Toke cleared his throat. "Joe, we found some graffiti on the exterior wall."

Joe's eyes narrowed. "What graffiti?"

"It was on the west side, out of line of sight of the road," Del said.

"That's been there a month." Maggie raked a hand through her hair. Had it really been four weeks since the ugly paint had appeared on the side of her little house?

"Did you report it to the police?" Joe asked.

"No. I didn't want the persons responsible to think I was scared. I had enough problems getting through to some of the teens as it was." But that hadn't stopped Paul from doing something about it. He'd been angry enough to march down to the youth center and ream every teenager unfortunate enough to stop by that day. Maggie would rather have let the matter drop, not risen to the bait.

"What does it say?" Joe asked.

Del glanced at Maggie. "'Go away, white woman.'"

Joe stared at Maggie, his lips tightening into a thin line. "Any idea who might have done it?"

"Could have been one of a dozen." A bucket of white paint still sat in the storage room waiting for her to cover the hateful words, but so much had happened since that day she'd completely forgotten.

Joe glanced at her. "I thought you had a rapport with them."

"Things change. Besides, it's a long story." One she was entirely too tired to get into. "Shouldn't we concentrate on finding Dakota?"

"That's what I'm doing." He softened his words with, "I need to know everything that's gone on in your life for the past few months, maybe even year."

"You mean since you've been gone?" Her gaze met his,

unwavering for a few long seconds before she dropped hers. What was the use? He had never loved her.

"Yes, since I left. With the kidnapping of your son following the accidental death of your husband, I wonder if Paul's death wasn't as accidental as we'd originally assumed."

Maggie struggled with the words teetering on the tip of her tongue. Would the facts she'd withheld make a difference in Joe's investigation, or would they only cloud the issue of finding her son?

When she didn't say anything, he continued. "Do you know if Paul was involved in any unusual activities?"

Gritting her teeth, Maggie shook herself and concentrated on Joe's question. He didn't need to know any more than he already did about Dakota. As the head of tribal police, he had a lot of influence within the tribe. It was enough for him to know his stepbrother's son was missing. "Unusual? What do you mean?"

"Was he acting strange, had he altered his habits? Did he hang out with anyone in particular?"

Maggie shook her head. "I don't know. Paul didn't tell me about his life outside our home." She swallowed against the lump rising in her throat. He hadn't told her because she hadn't let him. Paul had loved her and had married her when she'd been desperate. What had he gotten from the deal?

Nothing.

As the only white man she'd halfway trusted on the reservation, she'd gone to him to seek help in preserving her secret.

From the beginning, Paul knew Maggie still loved Joe but he'd married her anyway. Maggie had been the one to insist on a marriage in name only. Although Paul would have liked it otherwise, he'd abided by her wishes, agreeing to wait until after she'd given birth to persuade her otherwise. He'd slept in a separate bedroom down the hall from her, and he'd come and gone as he pleased. All this was information Joe didn't need to know.

No one knew. As far as the Painted Rock Indian Tribe was concerned, Paul was the father of her baby.

"He worked nights at the casino and I worked days at the youth center. We didn't see much of each other."

Joe's eyes narrowed. "Not much of a married life," he muttered, but he didn't ask any more questions about Paul's friends or activities. He turned to Officer Toke. "Check Paul's phone records and get out to the casino and ask around."

The officer nodded. "Will do." He tipped his head at Maggie. "Ma'am, let us know if you hear anything from the kidnappers."

A rush of panic pushed Maggie forward and she laid a hand on Joe's arm. "You have to find him, he's your—" She bit hard on her tongue until she tasted the bitter, metallic tang of blood. "—nephew," she finished in a rush. How close had she come to telling him the one thing she couldn't? Based on his belief that Indian children should be raised in the Indian culture, he wouldn't understand. He might demand custody of her baby if he knew Dakota was his son.

Chapter Two

While Officer Toke stood outside on her porch smoking a cigarette, Maggie paced her tiny living room more times than she cared to count, chewing through every last fingernail. Joe had gone to the police station with the others, promising to be back soon.

The more time that passed the more the walls seemed to close in around her. With Joe there, she could handle almost anything. Without him, she felt the black hole of loss sucking her down. She couldn't just wait around for his return, she had to do something to find her baby.

But who would have taken him? And why?

She sat on the couch and closed her eyes, focusing on everyone she'd been in contact with in the past six months. A person who could be malicious enough to steal a baby from his bed. It had to be someone who knew which room her baby slept in and that she would be the only adult in the house.

Who? Who? Who? She tapped her finger to her forehead. Faces swam in her mind of all the boys and girls she worked with at the youth center. She'd never invited any of them to her house, but one of them could have spied on her just as easily as someone had painted graffiti on her walls while she'd been away. As if her mind was on a continuous loop, she couldn't slow her thoughts enough to wrap around an individual. None of the teens surfaced as mean enough to steal her baby.

Was it even one of the teenagers she'd been working with? Could it be someone who knew Paul? If so, she was at a complete loss. For once, she wished she'd been closer to Paul than strangers in a shared house.

She pushed to her feet and strode to the window. When would Joe get back? He would know where to begin. He'd know who to question, who to call.

God, she prayed he did.

After one more circle around the living room, she stopped at the entrance to the hallway. From Dakota's doorway, light spread in a triangle on the carpet in the hall. As if drawn by an irresistible force, Maggie walked toward the room she'd avoided since the police left. The closer she got, the more her chest squeezed until she was gulping short, shallow breaths. The walls pressed in on either side of her. She didn't want to go in but she had to know, to see for herself, that her child really was gone.

This wasn't a dream.

The officers had tried to clean up their mess before they left, but she could still see the faint traces of dust from where they'd lifted fingerprints from the walls, windowsill and furniture.

Baby blankets and sheets had been stripped from the crib and sent to the state crime lab along with the blue cloud curtains that used to hang in the window. She'd made them herself from a piece of fabric she'd found in Rapid City last Christmas.

With an icy lump of pain lodged in her throat, Maggie struggled to breathe. Yet her eyes remained dry, almost too dry, with that achy, hollow feeling she couldn't blink away.

Longing to hold her child had become a physical need, just like breathing. And now that she was completely alone in her house, worry set in with a vengeance.

Was Dakota warm enough? Was he hungry? Were they changing his diapers and holding him so he wouldn't be afraid? She prayed whoever had taken her son wouldn't hurt him.

A sob rose in her throat and she pressed her fist to her mouth to keep from wailing aloud.

Then she noticed a powder-blue teddy bear lying forgotten against the wall. The plush, pillow-like toy was Dakota's favorite. He liked to sleep with it at night.

Maggie sank to her knees and gathered the plaything to her breast, inhaling the scents of baby powder and milk.

Why *her* child? He didn't like going with strangers, preferring only those he recognized, his mother and his caregiver, Mrs. Little Elk.

Please Dakota, don't cry too much. With all the child abuse and neglect she'd witnessed in the year and a half she'd been on the reservation, she hoped whoever had Dakota wasn't one of the abusers.

She pressed her face into the teddy bear, squeezed her eyes shut and sent a prayer to God and the Lakota spirits to help Joe find her son. At this point, she didn't care if he found out he was the father or if he sued for custody. Maggie loved Dakota so much she'd give him up to his father if she could be certain he was alive and taken care of.

Why hadn't she heard them when they'd entered her house? A good mother would have woken up at the slightest movement. If only she hadn't slept soundly. If only she'd woken with the dream. If only she'd left the reservation and gone home to Des Moines when Joe went to war. She should have left while she was still pregnant and Dakota was safe in her womb. Her baby would still be with her if she'd gone to Iowa. None of this would have happened.

If only.

She buried her face in the bear's soft nylon fur, her shoulders shaking, her body racked with dry, silent sobs. Alone in the middle of the prairie, her son was nowhere to be found.

The phone in her bedroom rang twice before Maggie heard it, so deep was she in her misery.

She lurched to her feet, the teddy bear still in her hand, and raced for the cordless phone on her nightstand.

"Hello?" She practically hyperventilated with her hopes and fears tangled in her chest.

"We'll trade the baby for what was stolen from us. Coyote Butte. Saturday, midnight. Come alone or we kill the kid."

"My baby? Is Dakota all right?" Maggie asked in a strangled whisper. "Please. Is he okay?"

An infant's cry could be heard in the background, before the line went dead.

"Dakota!" Maggie crushed the receiver to her ear, straining to hear her baby. Her hands shook so much she banged the phone against her temple, the pain barely registering. "Dakota! Oh, please, let me have my baby!"

"Maggie?"

As her vision blurred, the phone slipped from her ear. They had her baby and he was alive. Blackness curled around her and her knees buckled.

"Maggie!" Joe was there, gathering her into his arms, holding her up when her legs gave way. He smoothed her hair from her face and muttered soothing words.

She stood for several moments, reminding herself to breathe, telling her heart to go on beating, absorbing the strength, smell and touch of Joe holding her in his arms.

Finally, Joe tilted her chin up and stared down at her intently. "What happened, Maggie?"

"I heard my baby." Her fingers clutched at the lapels of his shirt. "They have Dakota. He's alive."

THANK THE SPIRITS. Joe held her face against his shoulder. "Shhh, he'll be okay." He hoped to hell they found the child before the kidnappers did something stupid. The tribal police were already combing through a list of possible suspects and the state police had issued an Amber Alert throughout South Dakota and the bordering states. The FBI would be there within the next two or three hours. For now, the best he could do was to hold Maggie and help her through the terror of her loss.

With her body pressed against his and the scent of herbal shampoo stirring his senses, memories flooded in.

It had been extremely hot the summer he'd first met Maggie. He'd hung around the activity center on the pretext of working out with the young people. What he wanted was information about drug abuse and drug dealing involving the teens. What he found was a pretty white woman playing a lousy game of basketball with the young adults. Sweaty, her hair curling wildly around her flushed face, she'd looked so alive, so vibrant. Joe couldn't resist hanging around. And she'd been so good with the kids, concerned and caring about everything in their lives.

Even after he identified the teens involved in the drug trafficking, he still went by the center with one excuse or another to talk to Maggie. His fascination for the auburn-haired social worker with the sunny smile was pretty obvious.

Charlie Tatanka, a recovering teen drug abuser, had agreed to assist in a DEA sting operation to bring the dealer in. Because of the rapport and level of trust he had with Maggie, the teen insisted she be close at hand as the bust went down.

Within the first two minutes of the maneuver, the dealer realized it was a setup and freaked, pulling a gun. Charlie was shot in the arm before the DEA and the tribal police could disarm the perpetrator.

Joe remembered how upset Maggie had been. As distressed as any parent would be over her own child, she'd accompanied the boy in the ambulance to the hospital where she'd stayed half the night ensuring Charlie was comfortable and had the proper treatment.

After the drug dealer was handed over to the state police, Joe dropped by the hospital to check on Charlie and Maggie. Charlie's father was there to take him home in his pickup truck. Joe offered to give Maggie a lift. That's when his inward struggle began.

She was still wired, talking nonstop during the trip back, riding an adrenaline high. Although worried about Charlie she couldn't contain her excitement over ridding the reservation of another dealer. Her cheeks were flushed and her eyes shining.

She'd been so beautiful, Joe had had a tough time concentrating on the road. When they'd arrived at Maggie's small house on the reservation, he'd insisted on checking out the place to make sure she was safe. Reluctant to leave her, he'd been caught up in her exuberance, the passion of her conviction spilling into him and kindling a similar passion of another nature.

When Joe started to leave, Maggie made the mistake of throwing her arms around his neck to thank him for caring about the teenagers. Unable to resist, he'd returned the embrace, kissing her until he was breathless, amazed at the burst of desire surging through his body.

In the heat of that embrace, he hadn't given a thought to what color, race or religion she was. That she wasn't Indian didn't cross his mind once. He only knew he had to hold her, touch her and feel her skin against his. The kiss didn't end until morning. He'd spent the night in Maggie's arms feeling as if he'd been given a gift from the spirits.

Then he'd woken to reality and a vast amount of guilt. He'd made a promise to his father that he'd continue the ways of his people. There was no room for a white woman in the Indian culture—no place for her in his promise to his father. He'd left that morning without a word, before she'd awakened.

He'd taken two days off from work and escaped to the bluffs on a vision quest, his mind a confused mass of old beliefs and fresh desire. The quest turned into a reaffirmation of his Lakotan beliefs, but he moved no closer to resolving his feelings for Maggie.

Nor would he be given the chance to work through them. Upon his return, the first thing that hit him was the

message on his answering machine from the South
Dakota National Guard. "You've been ordered to active
duty. You have twenty-four hours to report to your
assigned duty station."

His world had rushed in around him and he'd made a
decision. For the next fourteen months, he'd lived with the
result in the hell of Iraq.

But now he stood with Maggie once again in his arms
and knew what a terrible mistake he'd made. Her soft
curves had blossomed even more as a mother and he liked
it—almost too much. She was his stepbrother's widow,
still mourning the loss of her husband.

When Maggie stopped shaking, he held her away. "Are
you going to be all right?"

She sniffed and rubbed her nose against the sleeve of
her sweatshirt. "You must think I'm a complete flake."

"No, your son was kidnapped. I'd say you're reacting
the way any mother would."

"Thanks." A tentative smile lifted the corners of her mouth.
Then her eyes filled with more tears and her lips trembled.

Joe wanted to kiss those lips and chase away her fears,
instead he folded her into his arms. Her watery smile was
a sad reminder of the how happy she used to be. That
seemed like a lifetime ago. "I remember the first time I saw
you at the youth center. You were playing basketball with
some of the kids."

A hiccupping laugh was muffled against his shirt. "I
was terrible."

"No," He tipped her head up. "You were wonderful."

"How can you say that? I didn't even know how to
dribble."

"But you tried." She'd laughed and played, even though she couldn't bounce the ball once without having it taken away from her.

Maggie's lips twisted. "I never could get a ball in the bucket."

His arms tightened around her slim waist. "Yes, you did."

"Not by myself." Her voice dropped to a whisper and she tucked her head against his chest.

He'd helped her make a shot by standing behind her and placing his hands over hers. Her backside had pressed against him, stirring his blood in a way he couldn't ignore.

The warmth of Maggie against him now brought back those memories. His body remembered her shape and responded. Joe closed his eyes and willed the surge to subside. He wasn't there to make love to Maggie. "Who were you playing with? I can't remember."

"Charlie, Tray and Kiya…" She stopped her list and her breath caught.

Joe glanced down to see her eyes fill again with tears. "What?"

Her fingers curled in his shirt and she pressed her face against his chest. "Kiya was alive then."

Joe had received the news from Paul that Kiya Driskall, one of the troubled teens Maggie had been working with, had overdosed.

"What happened, Maggie?"

"I don't know." Maggie tore away from Joe and walked toward the window. "She'd been through detox at the hospital. She was doing so well." She inhaled a jerky stream of air and let it out, her shoulders bowing with her release. "Charlie found her behind the center, she'd injected meth. There was nothing we could do. She was already dead." Maggie turned to Joe, her eyes haunted.

"It wasn't your fault, Maggie." He reached for her, but she backed away.

"No, Joe." She jerked away. "I failed her. Just like I failed Dakota. I wasn't there when she needed me. The kids quit coming to the facility, even the ones that weren't involved in drugs or alcohol. They just quit coming. I ended up going to them. One by one. But no one would talk to me except Charlie and even he was afraid to be seen with me. It was like I was the plague."

Joe shook his head. "Don't blame yourself, Maggie. Something else must have happened." Possibly something related to Dakota's kidnapping?

"I don't know. I wish to hell I did." She turned back to the window and pressed her cheek to the glass. "Now Dakota's gone."

"He's not dead, Maggie. Don't give up on him." Joe stepped up behind Maggie and turned her toward him. "You ready to go to work on this case?"

For a moment she stared at him, her eyes glazed and unseeing.

She blinked, and the Maggie he remembered—the Maggie who could fearlessly stand up to a group of rowdy teenagers surfaced. "I'm ready."

Chapter Three

"That's my girl," he said.

Joe almost dropped his arms from around her at the words. She'd married his brother and had a kid as soon as he left. How could he wish Maggie was his girl? Then he looked into eyes so green they reminded him of prairie grass in springtime. He could see why Paul had fallen in love with her and offered to give her what Joe couldn't. Maggie was the kind of girl who was easy to love, if you didn't have a thick head.

During the time he'd spent hunkered down with his troops, with bullets and mortars flying overhead, he'd discovered what a fool he'd been. The soldiers he'd fought with were his brothers. Black, white, red—it didn't matter. They relied on each other to survive. They shared the same world, the same country. He wished he'd seen the truth before he left. Before Maggie had married Paul.

Her full lips drew into a thin line. "Where do we start?"

"First, let's get you out of here." He let go of her and walked back toward the living room. "Grab a coat, you're going to work with me."

She reached into a closet for a winter jacket, scarf and gloves, pulling them on before she paused to say, "What did they mean, give back what I stole? I didn't steal anything. At least not that I know of."

"That's what we want to find out. When we get to the station you can tell me everything you know about what's been going on on the Painted Rock Reservation and anything Paul might have been involved with at the Grand Buffalo Casino."

"That won't take long," she muttered.

He grasped her hand and gazed down at her. "Everything, Maggie. Even the smallest detail may be a clue as to what triggered someone to hold your baby for ransom."

"Okay," she said, not sounding convinced. She drew away from him, her chin down, making a show of fitting her gloves against her fingers.

Was she uncomfortable about sharing information with him?

Probably. He'd been a jerk before he'd left. What proof did she have that he wasn't still a jerk? A bitter lump of regret settled in the pit of his stomach. "Look, if it makes you feel any better, one of the other officers can interview you."

Her head came up, her eyes widening. "No. I want you." Was that trust in her eyes? Or was he mistaking desperation for something he wanted to see?

"Okay. But let's get out of here."

She glanced back at the living room, heaving a long sigh. "I want him back, Joe." The words had become Maggie's mantra, echoing inside Joe's thoughts.

He stared at the plain room with what looked like hand-me-down furniture. The faint scent of talcum powder and baby lotion permeated the air. The only bright spots in the room were the playpen in the corner and a few toys scattered on the couch cushions and the floor. A happy enough environment to raise a kid, missing only one thing.

The kid.

Joe's gut twisted and he wrapped an arm around Maggie's shoulders. "We'll find him."

"Alive?" she said, her voice a breathy whisper.

"Yes." If it was the last thing he did.

MAGGIE CLIMBED into the passenger seat of the SUV Joe used as his official tribal police vehicle. She felt funny, as though she was the criminal, even though the cage between the front and back seats was behind her. The thought angered her. Her house had been violated and her baby stolen, not the other way around. She jumped when the radio on Joe's shoulder squawked.

"Sorry." He flipped a switch on the device and it quieted.

Joe sat silent all the way to reservation police headquarters, a metal building with tan siding in the heart of the scattered community.

He climbed down and rounded the hood while Maggie sat with her hands clenched in her lap, her eyes staring out the windshield. As her mind replayed the message from the kidnappers, she tried to read into it any glimmer of a clue. But she came up with nothing.

He opened the passenger door and held out his hand.

Maggie turned to stare down at him. "Joe, Saturday is three days from now. I can't wait that long to find my baby."

"I know. That's why we're here. We're not waiting." He

helped her from the truck and walked her toward the building without removing his hand from hers.

The pressure of his big gloved fingers against hers, provided a little of the reassurance she so dearly craved. She needed it to keep her from stomping her feet in the gravel parking lot and screaming against the injustice. With every nerve sizzling beneath her skin she felt like a firecracker on the verge of exploding. *Where's my son!*

Once inside, Joe seated Maggie at his office and pulled a digital recorder, pad and pen from a drawer. "Let's start from the beginning."

Maggie listed off the names of the juveniles she'd worked with prior to Kiya's suicide.

"Can you think of any reason why she'd show up at the center after taking meth?"

"No. And the tribal police were clueless. It didn't make sense. If she was back on drugs after all everyone had done for her, I'd think she'd feel so guilty she'd hide in shame."

"Unless she realized her mistake and came back for help."

"A little too late." Maggie had thought of that, distraught that she hadn't been there for Kiya when she'd needed her most.

"I can't understand what went so wrong during the time I was gone." Joe tapped his pen against the metal desk.

"Things were different. The tribal police didn't have their leader. They tried to keep things together, but all I could figure was the teenagers were being influenced by an outside source."

Joe shoved a hand through his dark hair. "My deployment couldn't have come at a worse time."

Maggie almost snorted, but held her reaction in check.

You're telling me. She'd listened to the man she'd fallen in love with inform her they had no future. Then he'd walked away—or rather flown away—to the other side of the world. Two weeks later, she confirmed her suspicions, she was pregnant.

She gazed at the top of Joe's head as he bent to the task of noting her responses and her heart softened. Fourteen months had given her time to get over her anger and to learn more about this man through the people on the reservation. The more she learned, the more she understood the reasons for his reaction to their night of lovemaking.

Joe had lost his father when he was ten years old. Chaska Lonewolf had been a gentle man, proud of his heritage, proud of his son and determined to instill in him the ways of his ancestors. But he hadn't had the chance. He'd died while out hunting when his truck had flipped onto him.

The loss of Chaska Lonewolf as a husband and financial provider for the family had devastated Joe's mother. She'd taken Joe from the reservation, the only home he'd ever known, and gone to work in Rapid City, where she'd met and married Kevin Brandt. Shortly after the wedding, Kevin's ex-wife had dumped six-year-old Paul on the new family and left town.

School wasn't easy for a Native American boy in a white man's world, but Joe had kept his head low and studied hard, determined to return to the reservation and his way of life as soon as he was old enough. The time had come sooner than he'd expected when Kevin was laid off and once again the family was destitute.

They'd packed up their meager belongings and moved

back to the reservation where Kevin drank, bragged about Paul and berated Joe every chance he could get. A miserable life for a little boy who'd lost a loving father. No wonder he'd pushed Maggie away. What had the white man done for him besides give him pain?

Maggie felt deep compassion for the ten-year-old Joe. She'd struggled with the truth of Dakota's parentage. He deserved a father like Joe's. He deserved Joe. But Joe had spelled it out in his parting speech. There was no room in his life for her. So Maggie had to make arrangements to keep the tribe from knowing the baby was Joe's.

Her first instinct was to leave her job and run as far from the reservation as she could. But the teens she'd been working with needed her almost as much as her unborn baby. When Paul started coming around her work, flirting with her, she jumped at a solution.

As it turned out, Paul was the only one who'd known she was pregnant before she married him. He'd been patient, waiting for her to get over the man who got her in that condition. In love with her from the start, he waited throughout her pregnancy, showering her with encouragement and as much affection as she'd let him. But when the baby was born, the wall of her emotions for Joe still stood between them. Maggie wanted to love this man who'd stepped in and helped her in her time of need, but she couldn't.

Paul must have realized this because he spent more and more time working at the casino. Maggie never saw him. For the most part, she and Dakota were on their own.

Without her son, Maggie felt more alone in the world than ever. If not for Joe, she didn't know what she'd do.

AFTER MAGGIE'S INTERVIEW, Joe dropped her off at the youth center, despite his better judgment. She'd insisted, saying she needed time to check on her kids and to think.

He'd grabbed her hand before she slipped out of his vehicle. "Promise me you'll call if you need anything?"

"I will," she said, climbing down.

"I'll pick you up around three."

Her head jerked up and she stared at him, her eyes glassy as if she had to concentrate to focus. "No need."

A gentle smile lifted his lips. "You don't have your car here."

"Oh." She was preoccupied, and rightly so with her baby missing. "Okay." That was all she said before she turned and walked toward the building, pulling her coat tightly around her.

Joe wanted to go after her and coax her into telling him everything going on in her head. He felt like she was living detached from him and the world around them and he couldn't get through to her.

With his stomach knotted, he swung his SUV to the west, bumping along a rutted track that shouldn't be called a road by anyone's standards.

Fifteen minutes later, he pulled into a dirt driveway and sat for a moment, staring at the one-story clapboard house standing alone on a knoll. The yard was free of clutter with not even a bush to adorn the base of the building. Two naked cottonwood trees edged up out of the dead grass, a poor break against the bitter north wind.

A nondescript house for one of the most respected members of the Painted Rock Tribe. Matoskah, or White Bear, had been the tribal Medicine Man for as long as Joe could remember. His reputation for native cures for common physical ailments had Lakotans from towns scattered across the reservation traveling the lonely back roads to seek his help. But more than the cures for disease and sickness, people sought him out for spiritual healing.

And that was the reason for Joe's visit.

With the burden of a child's life weighing on his shoulders, Joe needed focus and a mind clear of emotions, memories and confusion.

A mind clear of Maggie.

How could he still be upset that she'd married another man? He'd told her to take a hike, that she had no place in the life of a Lakota. Of *this* Lakota.

What they had shared was lust—deep, powerful lust. Not enough to maintain a relationship, not on a reservation where poverty and destitution were the norm. For some of his people, lust might be enough. But he and Maggie were from two different worlds. She was white and Joe was a dark-skinned Indian, sworn to uphold the ways of his people and preserve the Lakota bloodline and traditions for future generations.

Memories and regrets punctured his soul the day of his stepbrother's funeral, when he'd seen what he could have had. Maggie and her baby—a family to call his own.

Shoving his shoulders back, he knocked on the faded door and waited in the cold. After one long minute, Joe stepped from the concrete stoop and strode around the house. In the backyard stood a dome-shaped structure. Vapor wafted in the bitter morning air, a hazy fog lifting from the taut hide stretched over arched willow branches.

A smile lifted the edges of Joe's lips. Only Matoskah

kept his sweat lodge erect year-round, when others were dismantled after powwow and tourist season ended. The buffalo hide, darkened with age and years of smoke, held the secrets, hopes and dreams of many Lakotans, divulged in the way of the ancients.

Joe hesitated to intrude on the shaman's meditation.

"Enter the womb of our people, Son of Lonewolf." Age did little to diminish the powerful voice of the tribe's trusted healer. And how did he always seem to know who stood outside the lodge?

Holding the flap of skin aside, Joe stooped to crawl like an animal into a den, the steam rising from the rocks embracing him. He squatted to the left of the entrance and let his eyes adjust to the light from the fire's coals and the little bit filtering through the thick skin overhead. Before the steam could escape, Joe turned to secure the flap, sealing the lodge.

Vapor swirled around him and he inhaled, accepting the surge of power that coursed through his veins. No matter how many times he'd been in a sweat lodge, he could count on that blanket of peace permeating his body and soul. Overdressed for tradition, he unzipped his coat as sweat beaded on his upper lip and forehead.

To the right of the entry, a hunched and wrinkled figure sat cross-legged, facing the coals and steaming rocks in the dug out center of the small space. Naked except for a meager loincloth, Matoskah sat staring at the glowing coals. The flap of supple deer skin was his one concession to modesty in the spiritual haven of his ancestors where the Indian was meant to be naked in the womb of the earth.

Joe reached out to grasp the spiritual leader's forearm. *"Mitaku oyasin, chante wasteya, nape chiyusa pe."* My relative, with a good heart, I shake your hand. The words brought back an image of his father sitting across a similar bed of steaming rocks from an eight-year-old Joe. He'd taught him that the words symbolized the importance of family and the completeness of the circle—only one of many lessons his father would teach him of the Lakota way of life, lessons he'd promised to pass on to his children and his children's children.

Matoskah grasped Joe's forearm in a firm grip. *"Hau kola."* Hello, my friend.

"Forgive me, Matoskah, for intruding on your reflection. I have need of your counsel."

The old man nodded and resumed staring into the coals.

Joe struggled to suppress his impatience. He felt out of place with too many clothes on his skin and too many thoughts churning in his head. But he forced himself to sit as the shaman did, drawing in a long, deep breath of the thick air. He closed his eyes, absorbing the souls of his ancestors, reaching for the combined wisdom of their years.

"What makes you as gray as the day outside, Joe Lonewolf?" Matoskah asked, the words swirling around the lodge like smoke from a peace pipe.

Joe opened his eyes and stared at the aged man. "A child is missing."

Without looking up from the bed of rocks, Matoskah's head dipped in a single nod. "I have heard."

"It's Maggie's child." Joe hadn't meant to say anything about Maggie, but there it was, blurted out like a teenager unable to think before he speaks.

"I understand."

What did the old man understand? Joe sat on his tongue,

afraid to open his mouth and spew forth more of his hurt and anger. He'd come to cleanse his mind, not to stir the air with his confusion.

"This woman is not of our people."

"No, she's not. She's one of the social workers with Indian Child Welfare Association. She works with the reservation teens."

The old man inclined his head. "I know of her."

As close-knit as the reservation was, Joe wasn't surprised.

"She's done well for our youth, working with those who abuse drugs and alcohol," Matoskah added.

"Yes." Maggie had thrown herself into her job, winning the hearts of many, including Joe. Had he not been so blind, they might have been together today.

"You must find this child."

"I know." The old man wasn't telling him anything he didn't already believe. Joe wanted him to tell him what to do about Maggie, but the question lodged in his throat.

"You fear you will fail?"

Was that it? Was he afraid he wouldn't find Maggie's baby? "Yes."

"Is your fear of failure for the child or for the woman?"

Joe leaned back. "The child, of course."

"And if you fail the child, you will not fail the woman?"

The answer was obvious, why would the shaman ask it? Joe dragged in a deep breath of the moist air, cleansing his nostrils and lifting the cloud from his head. "Yes."

"I sense hurt and resentment toward this Maggie."

Joe's chin dipped to his chest, his shame an almost overwhelming being seeping into his pores like the steam. "Yes." As if the haze cleared, Joe realized some of his confusion stemmed from his anger toward Maggie for marrying his stepbrother. "Will my anger cloud my judgment and ability to find her child?"

"Only you can know this. Do you mistrust her because she is not one of your people?" Matoskah had that uncanny way of reading Joe's thoughts before he'd completely formulated them himself.

"I did," Joe admitted, his softly spoken words drifting toward the ceiling with the stone vapor. After a year in the desert country of Iraq he'd come to realize he didn't trust himself where Maggie was concerned.

The shaman laid a hand on Joe's arm. "When you were in battle, did you care about the color of your soldiers? What religion, what race?"

Joe sat straighter. "No, they were my brothers."

"Does a child have a choice of what color, religion or race he is born into the world with?"

"You know they don't. But that doesn't change the world for our people on the reservation."

"We are all brothers, Joe Lonewolf." Matoskah lifted a cup of water and poured it onto the glowing stones. Steam hissed and rose in a cloud to fill the room. "Children are *wakanyega,* sacred beings. The child is one with the earth, one with our people, as is his mother. Look for this child like you would look for your own son, and remember, not all is as it appears. That is all you need to know. *Mitaku oyasin.*"

My relative.

Joe extended his hand and grasped his mentor's forearm. *"Pilamaya."* Thanks. Then on all fours, he crawled from the sweat lodge into the frigid air outside, welcoming the swift rush of cold filling his nostrils and stinging his cheeks.

Look for this child like you'd look for your own son. Dakota wasn't his son but he was a child, part of the circle of life and born of mother earth. His focus would be on finding the baby alive. Once he'd accomplished that mission, he could decide what to do about his feelings for Maggie.

Chapter Four

Maggie unlocked the door and entered, automatically reaching in to switch on the lights of the large gymnasium. Her snow boots made echoing clopping sounds as she crossed the painted concrete court to her office on the opposite side.

As she pushed the glass door open, a lump lodged in her throat. A colorful playpen stood in one corner as if waiting for her to place Dakota in it with his toys.

How many times had she brought Dakota to work with her? Had she set herself and her child up for this disaster? Had one of the teens who'd visited the center on multiple occasions seen Dakota and figured he'd be a good trade for something?

"Damn." Maggie slapped her hand to the doorframe and closed her eyes against the sting of tears. She could imagine Dakota crying for his mommy, holding out his hands for her to pick him up and make him safe. The tears squeezed through one at a time until she gave up and let them flow, hunching her shoulders in despair.

So caught up was she in her misery, Maggie barely

heard the sound of the outside door opening. When the sound of rubber boots stopped in front of her, she looked up into Winona Little Elk's dark face.

"Come, *thiblo*." Daughter. Heavy, warm arms curled around her shoulders and drew her into a maternal embrace.

"Oh, Winona, where is he? Where's my baby?" Maggie wailed into the older woman's wool jacket.

"I don't know. I miss him, too." Her shoulders shook with her own silent sobs and the two women stood holding each other until the storm passed.

After several minutes, Maggie pulled back and gave Winona a wobbly smile. "I'm sorry. I should be strong."

"Look at me," she snorted. "I'm just as bad." Winona's brown eyes were red-rimmed and puffy and she rubbed at the moisture clinging to the sunkissed, leathery skin of her cheekbones. "I love my *hoksika*." Little boy. Her words were a mix of English and the sometimes harsh, yet beautiful native Lakota language she'd grown up speaking with her parents and grandparents.

Maggie paced in front of the government-issued metal desk littered with files and work she'd thought so important only yesterday. Now nothing was as important as finding Dakota. She stopped and faced her son's caregiver. The woman who was more a grandmother, more than a babysitter to her child. "Why, Winona? Why would someone take my son?"

"Joe will find him and *ciks agli*." And bring your son home. Her voice rang with conviction as she stood with her back ramrod-straight and her ample shoulders pushed back. Winona's waist-length hair hung in long braids over her shoulders, the gray ropes a stark contrast to the black wool of her winter jacket. The woman was Lakota and her proud lineage shone through in her high cheekbones and deep-brown eyes. Then her shoulders slumped forward. "Do you think one of the tribe took *hoksika?*"

"I don't know anyone but the teenagers and people of the tribe. Who else would take him?" She hesitated for a moment and made a decision. "Winona, I had a call this morning from the kidnapper."

Winona's eyes widened and she reached for Maggie's hands. "What did they say? What did they want?"

Maggie's brows furrowed. "That's the problem. They want to use Dakota as a trade."

"A trade for what?"

"I don't know." She threw her hands in the air and turned away, searching her office for the answer and coming up blank. She sighed and faced Winona. "The man said something about trading Dakota for what was stolen."

"What do you mean, 'what was stolen'?"

"I wish I knew. I'd give it to them. Hell, I'd give them everything I own to get Dakota back."

Winona's eyes narrowed into a ferocious scowl and she tapped her finger to her chin. "What would someone want so badly they'd take our *hoksika?*"

"I've tried and tried to come up with something. But frankly, I don't have anything of value. And I certainly haven't stolen anything."

"You think the kidnapper is Lakota?"

"I think so. The meeting place is on the reservation at Coyote Butte." Maggie stepped behind her desk and sank into her battered office chair. "I don't even know where that is, much less what I supposedly stole."

The older woman shook her head. "I don't understand the ways of the young people of my tribe. Have they no shame? Drug use and alcoholism is a disgrace, child abuse unforgivable and that casino should never have been built."

"I thought the tribe was happy about the money the casino brings to the community."

Winona's lips thinned. "Money is not everything."

"Your husband, Tom, works there, doesn't he?" Having worked on the reservation for almost as long as the casino had been open, Maggie knew the benefits the tribe received from the profits. New roads, a new clinic and next year the new school would be complete. "What's wrong with the casino, other than the usual habitual gamblers?"

"Tom isn't sure, but he has the feeling there are illegal activities going on there. He just can't put his finger on it."

Maggie leaned forward. "What makes him think that?"

"He's a janitor, and as a janitor, he's somewhat invisible. He sees things." She shrugged. "That's all he will say."

"Do you think someone from the casino took Dakota?" Maggie pushed away from the desk and stood.

"I don't know."

"I've never been there, even when Paul was alive."

"Did Paul tell you anything about his work or the people there?" Winona asked.

"No." Maggie sat down again and buried her face in her hands. "I've made such a mess of my life. And poor Paul is dead."

"Does Joe know Dakota is his son?"

For a full five seconds, Maggie's heart stopped beating. When it started up again, it pounded against her rib cage, threatening to burst out with the force of her lie. Slowly, she lifted her head from her hands and stared at Winona. "How did you know?"

"Dakota may have your red hair, but he has the skin and eyes of his father's people."

Maggie jumped to her feet, and grabbed Winona's hands. "You won't tell anyone, will you?"

Pudgy brown fingers patted hers. "I won't tell what is not mine to tell. But why?"

"Joe didn't want me because I wasn't Lakota."

"That's ridiculous." Winona waved her hand around the room filled with pictures of the teens Maggie worked with on a daily basis. "You care about our children more than most of the people on the reservation."

"He said I didn't fit in his way of life. I didn't belong." She dropped Winona's hand and turned to the window overlooking the indoor basketball court.

"Men can say stupid things when they're going off to war. They aren't in their right minds." Winona's lips twisted. "If he'd known about the baby—"

"No!" The old hurt and fear surfaced and Maggie frowned. "I was scared. Afraid that if I told him about the baby, he'd take him away from me and raise him within the tribe. I'd lost Joe, I couldn't lose my baby as well." And if he'd decided to marry her, he'd have been doing it out of obligation, not love. She couldn't stand to be an obligation. She'd thought she'd be better off marrying someone else than being in love with a man who'd never love her in return.

"So you married Paul?"

"Yes." Maggie's chin tilted up. "I thought if I married Paul, everyone would think Dakota was his. I made him promise not to tell."

"What was in it for Paul?"

Paul. Dear, sweet Paul. Regret burned in Maggie's gut. In her attempt to protect herself and her son, she'd put Paul in the situation she most wanted to avoid. Paul had stepped in when she was desperate, but despite his love for her all she felt for him was platonic affection. She'd tried to sleep with him but couldn't, not with the knowledge she still loved her baby's father. He'd given up his chance to choose a woman who'd love him to help Maggie. And he'd died before she could make things right. "Paul loved me."

"You should tell Joe about Dakota. He has the right to know. Especially, since it's his son who's missing."

"I know." Maggie clasped her hands together, twisting the simple gold band around her ring finger. She'd insisted she didn't want a diamond engagement ring. A band was all that was necessary to keep her secret.

She slipped the ring from her finger and shoved it into her pocket. "You're right, Winona. I should tell him. But I want to be the one who tells him. Please don't mention it. The news should come from me."

"Yes. It should." Winona touched a hand to Maggie's cheek. "I promised Tom I'd fix lunch for him. Will you be all right alone? I could tell him to fix his own lunch."

"No. I'll be fine." Winona's offer to stay with her touched her. She'd made a few lasting friendships over the two years she'd worked at the reservation. Maggie trusted the older woman with her life and that of her son. She was the family Maggie didn't have.

"Call me if you need anything. Even if only for a shoulder to cry on, *thiblo.*"

"Pilamaya." Maggie responded with one of the few Lakota words she knew. Then she pulled the older woman into her arms and hugged her tightly, struggling to be strong when all she wanted to do was curl into a fetal position and cry. "I miss my baby."

"I know, I know." Winona patted her back once more and then held her at arm's length and said, "Trust him." After a long hard look, the old Lakota woman left.

The empty gym echoed with the sound of the outside door closing behind her. A blast of icy wind filtered across the concrete floors to send a chill across Maggie's skin. She wrapped her arms around her middle, shivering, and wondered if Dakota was warm enough.

The door screeched open and Maggie looked up, half hoping Joe would walk through. Her hopes died when Leotie Jones slipped through and advanced across the concrete with her high-heeled boots grating against the silence. "Oh, good, you're here," was her only greeting. No How are you? or Hello.

Maggie squeezed her eyelids shut for a moment and willed Leotie to go away. *I don't need this. Not now.* Then she opened her eyes and forced herself to be pleasant, something that wasn't easy around the self-centered woman. "Leotie," she said, dipping her head in acknowledgement.

"I just stopped by to tell you how sorry I was about your baby." She cinched the belt circling the waistline of her long, black leather jacket.

"Thanks." She couldn't help it that the one word implied anything but gratitude. Leotie had had it in for her from the first day Maggie had set foot on the reservation. Or should she say from the first day she'd run into Joe Lonewolf and instant attraction had practically ignited the dry prairie grass all around the youth center? Leotie considered Joe her territory and saw Maggie as an encroaching outsider. She'd done everything in her power to get between Maggie and Joe and spoil any chance of a blossoming relationship.

"I was hoping we could forget about the past and, you know, let bygones be bygones, and all that." Leotie stared around Maggie into her office. "Aren't you going to invite me in?" Although her words sounded cheerful, the slight curl of her lip indicated she wasn't impressed with the sparse furnishings or the two hard plastic chairs positioned in front of Maggie's desk.

"Normally, I would. But there's nothing normal about the way I feel today." She stared hard at Leotie, hoping she'd get the message and leave. "Leotie, I'd rather be alone."

"I see." Leotie's forced smile turned into a sneer and she crossed her arms over her ample chest, flipping her red-streaked black hair over her shoulder. "Joe's working the case, isn't he?"

This was more Leotie's style—cut to the chase. Maggie braced herself for the attack. "Yes, Joe's working the case."

"You know he'll never marry you, don't you?"

"I didn't ask him."

"Well, don't." Her eyes narrowed. "He won't ever marry you. He has too much of his father in him to care about a white woman."

"I said, I didn't ask him." If Leotie didn't get the hell out soon, Maggie was afraid she'd say or do something she'd regret. She had to remind herself not to rise to

Leotie's bait, to take the high road. But her emotions were raw and she wasn't in the mood.

Mentally, she counted to ten.

One.

"If he marries, he'll choose a Lakota woman."

Two.

"Like me."

Three.

"Do we understand each other?"

Four-five-six-seven-eight-nine-ten! "Leave, Leotie." Maggie pointed to the door, her lips set in a firm tight line, afraid if she opened them again, she'd spew forth venom.

"Fine." Leotie tugged at the belt of her already tight coat and flipped her hair back again. "Just remember—"

Maggie's control snapped. "Out!"

Leotie snorted and spun on her heel, marching to the door. But she couldn't leave without a parting shot. "Just because he's helping you doesn't mean anything."

With her tongue pinched between her teeth, Maggie only pointed to the door.

Leotie flung the heavy metal door open and it crashed against the building, bouncing back to smack into her shoulder. She swore and shot a glance backward as if to see if Maggie had seen her fit of temper backfire.

Served her right. The bitch didn't know what love was. Joe deserved someone who really cared for him and the people of his tribe. Not a venomous witch like Leotie, who only cared about herself. He needed someone kind, caring and devoted to his people.

Someone like you? A niggling voice asked the question in Maggie's head.

No. Not a red-headed white woman.

Best stick to worrying about Dakota. Joe was out of reach.

She walked into her office and closed the door.

As soon as Joe entered the station he asked, "Any leads from the Amber Alert?"

"A couple of sightings of women carrying babies into stores in Rapid City." Del shrugged. "The babies were theirs."

"Do you have anything on the graffiti on Mag—Mrs. Brandt's house?" Her married name burned an acid path down his throat and gave him the worst case of heartburn he'd known since returning from Iraq.

Del slid a sideways glance at him, a smile quirking the corner of his mouth. "Bother you that she married Paul after you left?"

"No," Joe lied. Hell yes, it bothered him. The tarmac hadn't even cooled from the plane taking off before she'd married Paul.

What galled him most was who she had married.

His stepbrother.

Paul had been nothing but a thorn in his side since his mother had married Kevin Brandt. The six-year-old boy had followed him around like a lost puppy, mimicking his every move.

Now that Paul was gone, Joe realized how much he missed his stepbrother and had to admit he'd enjoyed the hero-worship when they were younger.

"What makes a woman go out with one man and marry another the next day?" Del asked, and then winced. "Sorry, that's pretty personal."

"She had the right."

"I thought you two would make a go of it before you left."

"Well, we didn't." Joe moved through the crowded office to his desk in the corner and stared down at the neat top, as yet uncluttered with a full workload. He'd been easing back into his old job as chief of tribal police. Until today. The kidnapping had thrown him full-force back into work. "Did you find out who left the graffiti on her house?"

"Not yet. I bet it's one of the druggies that hangs out with the Sukas Gang. My inside source says one of them has a gripe against your Maggie for the death of his girl-friend, Kiya Driskall."

The Sukas Gang had been growing before Joe had left for his tour of duty, but he'd thought their numbers man-ageable and somewhat contained. And from the police report, Kiya's death had been attributed to drug overdose. "Kiya's death wasn't Maggie's fault."

"We know that, but for some reason Randy Biko hasn't figured that out."

"Randy? I thought he'd turned around and straightened up his act?"

Del shrugged. "A lot changes in a year."

"Apparently." Not for the first time that day, Joe regret-ted the timing of his call to service with his South Dakota National Guard unit. He wondered if things would have been different if he hadn't gone. Would he have turned his back on Maggie? Would Kiya Driskall still be alive? Would the gangs have expanded whether or not he'd been here? He'd never know.

One thing was certain, he didn't regret his time in Iraq. The people of that country needed someone to defend their right to life and the men in his unit had needed him.

Courting death in Iraq taught him a lot about himself. And if he could he'd take back what he'd said to Maggie before he left.

Del strode to the wall where a white board hung, littered with notes from previous cases. He wiped it clean and wrote in black erasable marker the date and time of the missing person report and the call. "We know it's a kidnapping and we've been given the ultimatum. We need to find what it is they think was stolen," Del said.

"What we need to do is find the baby before they hurt him." Joe pushed his chair back and stood. His heart pinched in his chest at how devastated Maggie would be if Dakota was hurt or killed. "Call in the entire force, we're going house-to-house across the reservation until we find that kid. Do the necessary calling. I'll be back in a minute."

"Where you going?"

"I'm going to get Maggie. She'll want to be there for the search."

"Yes, sir!"

Joe left the office, his long stride eating up the distance between the door and his vehicle. He hated himself for the way his pulse quickened at the thought of seeing Maggie again. He shouldn't be feeling that way for a newly widowed woman. Hell, she'd only lost her husband less than two weeks ago.

FOUR HOURS LATER, the sky was dark except for the yellow glow of porch lights on Red Feather Street. Disappointment gnawed at Joe's gut. They were no closer to finding Dakota. Joe pulled the SUV to a stop in Maggie's drive.

She sat for a moment staring at her house. What was she thinking?

Joe couldn't imagine the worry going through her mind. "We'll find him, Maggie. We still have the scattered homes farther out to check."

She turned to him and placed a hand on his arm. "You'll call me if you find anything? It doesn't matter what time of day or night. Please call me."

Her eyes beseeched him in the light from his dashboard, the pale purple smudges beneath them a testimony to the long day and the little sleep she'd had the night before. Joe couldn't stop his hand from reaching out to cup her chin. "I'll call you, Maggie. You know I will. I want Dakota back, too. He's part of my family."

Maggie's eyes widened before her lids dropped down to cover the shock in their smoky-green depths. She jerked her chin from his grasp and fumbled with the door handle. "I should go inside. Maybe the kidnappers left another message on my answering machine."

Had he imagined that look of fear when he'd mentioned Dakota was family? Did she hate him so much that she didn't want him to be a part of her son's life? "Dakota's my nephew, Maggie. Does it bother you that I care about him?"

"No, not at all." She gathered her purse and pushed open the door.

She wasn't telling him something, and Joe wondered if what she held back was important to the case. He'd opened his mouth to ask her, when he noticed a movement out of the corner of his eye. His attention swung to the blinds in one of the windows. They hung at an odd angle. "Did you leave those blinds like that?" He pointed toward her house.

"Huh?" Maggie's gaze followed the direction he indicated. "No. That's the master bedroom. I never touch the blinds." She jumped out of the SUV.

"Wait, Maggie." Joe was out and beside her before she reached the front door. He set her to the side of the entryway and checked the handle. The door was locked securely. "Come on." He grabbed her hand and ran around to the back door.

The door stood wide open, the frame splintered from a harsh blow. "Someone kicked this door in," Joe said, his voice a low rumble in the dark.

"You think they're still inside?" Maggie whispered.

"I don't know, but I'm going to find out." Joe held her by the shoulders and stared down into her eyes, barely discernible in the light from the stars. "Stay here."

Chapter Five

Maggie waited in the dark of the back porch, her heart pounding so loudly in her ears she felt light-headed. Her imagination ran through every conceivable scenario from someone lurking in the shadows of the bushes to a killer waiting to take Joe down inside the house.

When she heard a crash, Joe's grunt and then a muttered curse, her heart skidded to a stop. She didn't hesitate, didn't stop to think about what she was doing—she entered through the broken door and flipped on the light switch.

Standing amid overturned chairs, Joe shot a frown at her. "I told you to wait outside. Go on." He didn't wait for her response, instead he slipped around the corner of the little kitchen and down the hallway.

The longest thirty seconds of her life stretched in front of her as Maggie held her breath.

Then Joe appeared in front of her. "Whoever broke in is long gone." His brow furrowed and he reached out to grab her shoulders. "You okay?"

Breathe, Maggie. She stared up into dark eyes and shook her head. "No, I'm not."

"Come here." Strong arms circled her and pulled her against the rock-solid muscles of his chest. "It'll be okay."

Anger pierced the wall of fear and Maggie pushed against him until he held her at arm's length. "How? How will it be okay if Dakota never comes home or you get hurt in the process of finding him? How could it possibly be okay?" Her voice faded from a shout to catch on a whispery sob and she leaned her forehead against the supple leather of his black jacket. "What happened? Why can't I figure this out?"

"I don't know," he said, stroking his hand down the center of her back like a parent comforting a frightened child.

Maggie shivered. The cold creeping in through the open back door spread throughout her system until her entire body shook.

"You're chilled." He set her away from him and moved to the back door, closing it as best he could. "You got a hammer?"

"B-b-beneath the s-sink," she said, her teeth chattering against each other so hard that surely they'd chip.

Joe glanced from the door to her. "Go get in bed and cover up. I'll be right there."

Shaking uncontrollably, barely able to walk a straight line, Maggie did as she was told and stumbled through the wreckage to her bedroom. The mattress was stripped of the bedding and lay crossways over the box spring. Pillows were ripped to shreds, the fluffy stuffing littered the floor and every dresser drawer lay scattered or broken on the cheap carpet.

Clapping a hand over her mouth, Maggie stifled a moan, then she let go and crumpled to her knees, her body racked with tremors and sobs. Despair set in, sinking her down to a dark and shadowy place. Why? Why take Dakota? Why destroy her home? What could she have possibly done to deserve this?

Joe's hammering at the back door stopped, but Maggie's tears continued to flow unchecked until a pair of strong hands lifted her to her feet.

"Shhh, baby. Come here, let me warm you." He let go of her long enough to unzip his jacket and pull her in to share the warmth of his coat's sheepskin lining and his body, radiating heat she couldn't get enough of.

With a deep breath, Maggie inhaled the clean leather-and-aftershave scent of Joe. She laid her cheek against his heart, its steady thumping calming and exciting all at once. Pressing closer to his heat, she was frustrated by the clothing between them. If she could get past the layers of fabric down to the skin, she knew she could thaw the chill threatening to overwhelm her.

Her fingers fumbled at the buttons of his shirt, loosening them one by one, the job made more difficult by the tremors shaking her frame. She had to touch his skin, feel how alive he was to know life was worth living, worth fighting to keep on going.

His hand stopped hers as she reached for the button at the top of his waistband. "You don't know what you're doing, Maggie."

Her hands slipped beneath the edges of his parted shirt across the coarse hairs sprinkled across his chest. "Hold me, Joe. I need to feel you close. I'm so cold."

He gripped her hands in his and set her away.

A lump lodged in Maggie's throat and she struggled to breathe past it. What was she doing throwing herself at a man who could never love her? Did she have no self-respect?

Joe moved around the room, righting the furniture and making the bed with clean sheets.

In a stupor, Maggie watched, her cheeks flaming at his second rejection of her. Well, she wouldn't do it again. She'd been stupid to make a move on him after he'd told her he wasn't interested. She wasn't stupid enough to do it again.

Anger stiffened her back and she bent to retrieve the faded comforter lying in a tangled wad on the floor, spreading it over the sheets.

As she smoothed her hand over the floral print, an image of Joe lying among the sheets in the king-size bed in his house flashed in her memory.

Molten blood rose from her core upward, spreading through her chest and up into her face, chasing away the bone-chilling cold. She dared a glance at Joe and regretted it instantly.

His gaze consumed her, his brown eyes smoldering in the dim lighting. "Who are we trying to fool, anyway?" He yanked her against him, his lips descending to grind against her mouth, his tongue lashing out to twine with hers.

When they finally came up for air, Maggie fell into Joe, her lips caressing the firm line of his jaw, her hands parting the fabric of his shirt. With shaking fingers, she threaded through the hairs covering his chest and angling down toward his belt. The jacket went first, sliding from his shoulders to land with a soft whoosh on the floor. The uniform shirt followed the jacket and Joe stood in his tan trousers and boots, bare-chested.

God, he was beautiful. Maggie pressed a kiss to his jaw. He tasted of salt and a hint of aftershave. She tasted again and then circled her arms around his neck and pulled him toward the bed. She needed him to hold her through the night, fill her until she felt alive, and love her like there was no tomorrow.

THEY WERE TOGETHER, in her bedroom, and she wanted him. Joe didn't stop her from kissing him and running her fingers over his body. Instead he gave back, kiss for kiss, thrusting his tongue into her mouth, unable to stop himself. Maggie felt right in his arms, like coming home to a fresh green meadow after a long hot stint in the desert. He drank her taste, felt her soft skin beneath his rough hands, drowning in her femininity.

Caught in the heat of a passionate web, Joe was drawn across the floor toward the bed. The bed Maggie had shared with his stepbrother. The stepbrother who'd only been dead for two weeks.

A cold blast of reality hit him square in the gut and he stopped. Stopped kissing, stopped smoothing his hands through her wavy, red hair. But he couldn't stop the way his heart squeezed in his chest. "I should go." He stepped backward until his hands fell to his sides.

"Why?" She shook her head from side to side as if in slow motion. "Did I do something wrong?"

"No. I just can't do this." His gaze fell on the bed behind her.

She looked from him to the bed and back, a frown creasing the skin on her forehead.

"Paul's only been dead for two weeks. This would be wrong."

Her frown cleared and she nodded. "Joe…Paul never slept here."

"What?" He'd been ready to leave, but her words held him captive. "What do you mean he never slept here?"

"He slept in the room on the other side of the kitchen. I slept here. Alone."

"What about Dakota?"

"That's just it." Maggie turned and walked away as far as she could get without actually leaving the room. Then she turned to face Joe. "Joe, there's something you should know about Dakota…. He's—"

A loud crash, like the sound of glass shattering, sounded down the hall toward the living room. Joe leaped across the room and pushed Maggie to the floor. "Stay here. And I mean stay."

He left the room in a crouching jog, switching the lights off in the hallway before he ran down its length. The steady beat of his heart against his eardrums was the only sound he heard as he made his way into the living room. When he reached the front door, an engine roared and tires screeched halfway down the street. By the time he ripped the door open, the vehicle had rounded the corner and disappeared.

"Damn." Joe yanked the cell phone from the clip on his belt and hit the speed-dial button for the station. "Linda, this is Joe Lonewolf. Where's Ben?"

Linda Brown Bear, the night dispatcher, answered, "He's cruising Highway 8 about five miles west of town."

"Damn." A movement from the hallway caught his attention.

Maggie stood in the entrance to the living room, staring at the broken window. Her face was drawn and anxious and her hands twisted together.

Joe's chest tightened at her obvious fear. He wanted to go to her and take her in his arms and shield her from all the ugliness of the past day. Turning to the side so he could only see her in his peripheral vision, he finished his call. "Linda, we just had a rock thrown through Maggie's window on Red Feather Street. A vehicle took off, but I couldn't get a license number or make on it. I don't know if this is the same person who broke into her house recently, but tell Ben to keep a regular surveillance through the neighborhood. And tell him to drop by and collect the evidence."

"Sure thing. I'll get right on it."

Joe could hear Linda's voice making the radio call to Ben even as she hung up the telephone.

Maggie had entered the living room and stared at the fist-sized rock that had shattered the front window. Then, piece by piece, she lifted the shards of glass into her open palm.

When she reached for the rock, Joe put out a hand to stop her. "Leave the rock where it is. We might get a set of prints off it." Joe let go of her arm. "You got a vacuum?" he asked.

"In the hall closet," she said, without looking up.

After thoroughly vacuuming the old carpet, he found a piece of plastic and taped it over the jagged hole in the window to stem the flow of cold air into the room.

Maggie was still crouched on the floor, her gaze intently searching. "Can't leave any glass. Dakota will be crawling soon." Her voice caught and she hunched over, her shoulders shaking with the force of her silent sobs.

Joe pulled her to her feet and into his arms.

"He'll come back, won't he?" Maggie asked, lifting her tear-filled gaze to his.

"Yes, Maggie. We'll get him back." He pulled her into

his arms and held her tight, hoping to hell he was right. She loved her son, that much was obvious. "You need to get some sleep. Dakota will need his mother to be well-rested when he comes home."

He led her back down the hallway to her bedroom. "Go on, get into your nightclothes. I'll go check the doors and windows."

After his deputy collected the evidence and left, Joe took his time checking through the house, combing over the small building for any clue as to what the kidnappers might want. He entered the bedroom on the far side of the kitchen, feeling like an intruder into someone else's private space.

The bed was neatly made with a plain blue bedspread. One picture sat on the chipped and dented dresser against the wall. Joe recognized it as one taken on a family camping trip to the Black Hills. Ten-year-old Paul stood next to Joe, each boy with a hand on the stringer of fish dangling between them. They'd caught fifteen trout that day on the river.

Joe could feel the edges of his lips curl upward. He hadn't thought about that day in a long time. Despite his determination to dislike his stepbrother, he'd had fun that day. They'd never been closer.

The smile drifted south and Joe turned away. Paul had only wanted him to like him and to accept him as his brother. But Joe had it stuck in his head that the only brothers he had were his Indian tribe. And Paul was a white boy interloper.

Regret burned like acid in his belly. It had taken his deployment to Iraq to open his eyes to reality. *We're all in this world together. All brothers in this life.* He wished he could have made things right before Paul had been killed in the car accident.

At least he could make it right by safely returning Paul's son to Maggie.

His search through the house yielded nothing of any great value or interest. When he reluctantly made his way back to Maggie's bedroom with the intention of leaving he stopped in the doorway, hesitant to expose himself to the temptation that was Maggie.

She lay on her back, the covers pulled up to her chin, her eyes wide and haunted. How could he leave her alone after everything that had happened?

"Is there anyone you can call who could stay with you tonight?" he asked.

Maggie shook her head. "I don't want to bother anyone."

"I can't leave you here alone."

"Then stay with me."

He inhaled and blew out a long stream of air. "I shouldn't."

"I promise not to touch you," she said, her lips curving into a pleading smile.

"It's not a good idea." Her touching him didn't concern him as much as his desire to touch her.

"I understand." She inched even lower in the bedclothes, such a small person alone in a house that had been violated.

"Okay, I'll stay. But I'll sleep on the couch." He couldn't stay in Paul's room with the memories so fresh and Dakota's room only had a crib.

"Will you stay in here until I go to sleep? You could sit on the bed for a while."

He could tell by the quiet tone that it took a lot for her

to ask. Heaving a sigh, he crossed the room and sat on the opposite side of the bed from her. "Sure."

Maggie turned toward him. "Thanks."

With her auburn hair spread across the white pillowcase, it was all Joe could do not to reach out and run his fingers through it like he had the night they'd spent together. "Just go to sleep," he said, his voice a little more harsh than he'd intended.

"Yes, sir." She reached out and placed her hand over his, forgetting her promise not to touch him. Her eyes drifted closed.

Joe's fingers curled around hers.

"Any idea who supplied the drugs to Kiya?" he asked.

"No," she said. With her free hand, she smothered a huge yawn. "The kids are closed-mouthed about it."

Several minutes of silence went by and Maggie's breathing became slow and even.

She was every bit as beautiful as she'd been on the night they'd made love, if not more so. Motherhood had rounded out some of her curves and added fullness to her breasts. But she was still the same Maggie who'd captured his attention with her fierce loyalty to the teens at the center and her desire to make their lives better.

The teens needed her. Hell, she belonged here. Perhaps more so than some of the full-blooded Indians who drank away their lives and beat their children.

Why hadn't he seen it before he left?

"Why did you marry Paul?" he whispered.

Maggie rolled to her back, taking Joe's hand with her. With her eyes closed and her voice a soft hush in the night, she muttered, "It's what you expected."

Her words reflected his own revelations about his relationship with Maggie. He'd failed her once. Would he fail her again?

As the red-haired woman next to him slipped into a deep sleep, Joe tried to pull his hand free of hers. He needed to sleep on the couch, away from her sweet smell and warm body. Out of reach of her natural allure.

But her fingers held tightly to his and Joe finally settled his back against the headboard and prepared for a long night of sleeplessness.

SMOKE SWIRLED AROUND *the interior of the ancient sweat lodge, blurring his view. He could make out only the silhouettes of others gathered around the circle of stones.*

Joe sat naked as was the way of his ancestors, staring into the glowing coals. He didn't recall coming to the lodge, nor did he remember removing his clothing. "Why am I here?" he asked into the void.

Silence curled around him in the tendrils of steam rising from the rocks. A faint whisper of voices reached out to him chanting, "Not all is as it appears."

Fog thickened until he couldn't breathe, and he heard the faint cry of a baby. As the crying increased in volume and intensity, Joe cried out, "Where are you? I can't see you."

The frightened cries wrenched at Joe's heart. He wanted to pluck the baby from danger and give him back to his mother to calm his fears, but he couldn't see through the dense mist. The shadowy figures seated in the circle swayed closer, like the essence of his ancestors pressing in at him until Joe's lungs felt as if they would burst. He gasped for air, feeling his head lighten and his thoughts dim.

Matoskah's voice rang low and clear in the fog, his words reverberating off the taut buffalo hide of the structure. "A child is one with the earth mother. Joe, you can not fail him."

The specters eased back and faded into the haze. Although they were gone from sight, Joe could still sense their presence in his soul.

He couldn't fail the baby, he couldn't fail his ancestors. He wouldn't.

On his knees, Joe searched desperately inside the low-ceilinged structure, unable to find the baby or the others whose shadows had wavered in the mist. The sweat lodge was empty except for him. When he found the entrance, he crawled through, burst into the frigid night air and stood straight on the South Dakota plains. Free of the choking fog, he breathed deeply, his head clearing, drinking in the view around him. Moonlight shed an eerie blue glow over the frozen land.

No baby could be seen or heard...and he stood alone.

Chapter Six

An electronic ringing pierced the fog of Maggie's sleep. Wishing it would go away, she tried to roll to her back, but something held her still.

Her eyes opened and she struggled to focus in the semi-dark of predawn. When her vision adjusted, she gasped.

A smooth dark arm draped over her hip and something warm cocooned her from behind. Or rather, someone.

Moving carefully, Maggie glanced over her shoulder.

She lay pressed into the curve of Joe's body, her back warm against his bare chest, her bottom snug against his— Heat filled her cheeks and spread throughout her body. How long had she been wrapped in his arms? All night?

For a moment she let the warmth fill her and lift her up from the worry of the day before, but the harsh ringing burst through the cocoon of Joe's sleep.

He jerked awake, rolled away and grabbed his cell phone from the nightstand. "Yeah."

Was it someone calling about Dakota? Had they found her son? Maggie sat up and strained to hear the other side of the phone conversation. Her heart beat a jagged rhythm in her chest and her hand rose to Joe's arm.

"Damn." He pushed to his feet and ran a hand through his hair. "I'll be there in ten. What about Tom?" He listened another minute, his lips pressed into a grim line. "Okay. I'll be there." He closed his cell phone and reached for the wrinkled uniform shirt lying on the floor. "Bernie Two Eagles was found in a ditch this morning."

Maggie gasped. "Is he…"

"Dead," Joe finished in a flat, emotionless tone. But the lines around his eyes seemed more sad.

She let out a long slow breath, her stomach turning over in her empty belly. "What happened?"

"Looks like gunshot wounds." As he buttoned the shirt, he stared across at Maggie. "I don't like what's happening around here."

"Me either." She shook her head then ventured the question burning in her mind. "Any news of Dakota?"

Joe frowned, his gaze soft on her. "Sorry."

She heaved a sigh and flung the covers aside. "I'm going with you."

"No. I'll be standing out in the cold investigating a crime scene all morning. You need to stay close to town. I'll have officers continue their door-to-door search."

"I can't sit around doing nothing." And she didn't want to be left alone to think about all the possible outcomes of the scenario playing out.

"Then visit the hospital. Tom Little Elk was injured as well in what appears to be a drive-by shooting."

A lump lodged in her throat. So that was the Tom he'd mentioned in his phone call. "I'd better get over to Winona.

I bet she's a wreck." She started unbuttoning her pajama top and got halfway down the line of buttons when she felt the heat of Joe's gaze sizzling across the exposed V of her breasts.

A thrill of awareness raised the temperature in the room by ten degrees. Deciding it better to complete her dressing in the bathroom, she grabbed jeans and a warm sweater from her closet.

Joe shrugged into his jacket. "I'll check with you later. You'll be carrying your cell phone, won't you?"

She stood in the bathroom doorway and nodded, holding her clothing like a shield against her chest. "Be careful, will you?" If something happened to Joe…

"I'm not the one being threatened." He leaned over and kissed her forehead. "Be careful."

Her stomach flipped again and the spot on her forehead where his lips had rested tingled. She gulped and forced words out. "If you hear anything on Dakota, you'll let me know?"

He stared straight into her eyes, his intense, deep-brown gaze unblinking. "You know I will."

"Joe?" Her hand reached out to touch his arm briefly before it dropped to her side.

"Yes, Maggie."

Her head dipped until she was looking at his feet, not his face. "Thanks for staying with me last night."

He stood for a moment without saying anything.

Maggie glanced up, half afraid of what she'd see in his face.

His thumb traced the line of her cheek and a smile curved his lips. "My pleasure," he said and left.

The ensuing silence cloaked the little house in an

ominous shroud. Maggie dressed quickly for her trip to the reservation clinic. Without Dakota to look after, she felt as though part of herself was missing. No baby noises cooed from her son's crib. She missed smiling and talking to him as she dressed him for his morning ride over to the simple, framed cottage Winona shared with her husband. He loved going to stay at Winona's. She was his grandmother, if not in blood, then in spirit, and he greeted her every morning with outstretched arms and a smile. He'd be sitting up soon and before Maggie knew it, Dakota would be crawling all over the place, getting into things and pulling up to stand.

Her throat clogged with the tears she'd sworn she wouldn't shed today. The police were conducting a house-to-house search on the reservation. FBI agents were working with them to profile the kidnappers and come up with possible suspects.

Racking her brain for who could have done this had only produced a monster headache, so Maggie decided to show her support to her friend and surrogate family member Winona Little Elk in her time of need. Maybe the visit would take her mind off Dakota, if only for a while.

She snorted. Like she could quit thinking about her son. *Not a chance.* She'd quit breathing before she quit thinking of Dakota with his chubby cheeks and soulful dark eyes.

With one last glance around the mess of her house, Maggie grabbed her purse from the counter and hurried across the living room to open the front door.

A teenager wearing a green-and-black army jacket burst through, knocking her out of the doorway and into the back of the couch.

"What the—" Struggling to get her feet under her and not topple over the back of the sofa, she didn't have time to be afraid before she recognized the culprit. "Charlie?"

Charlie Tatanka turned and slammed the door shut. "I'm sorry, Mrs. Brandt. I had to get in fast." The teen turned to her and gave her a worried smile. "Did you know your back door is nailed shut? I tried to get in through there, but it wouldn't open, even when I jimmied the lock."

"Yes, I know my back door's nailed shut." She shook her head. "That doesn't excuse the way you burst into my home."

"I know, I know." He only half paid attention to her admonishment as he peeked through the metal blinds over the windows. "I didn't know if they were following me."

"Who?" Maggie straightened and retrieved her purse from where it had fallen to the floor, trying hard not to appear alarmed in front of Charlie.

"The Sukas." He let the blinds go and sighed. "I shouldn't have come here."

"No, you shouldn't have. You know I don't allow the kids from the center to come to my home. My cell phone is always on and I'm more than willing to set up a meeting place, preferably at the center." She worked hard to keep her personal life separate from her work, especially since Dakota's birth.

"I couldn't meet you at the center." He jammed his hands in his pockets. "They'd see me."

"The Sukas?" Maggie walked to the window and lifted a slat of the blinds, peering out.

"Yes."

Everything appeared normal on the quiet street. Other than that her child was still missing, someone had broken into her house the night before and a teen had forced his way in this morning. Normal, ha! "Why are you afraid of the Sukas?"

A typical teen, Charlie shrugged as though it was nothing, but she could tell by the strain around his eyes that it was a lot more than nothing. "They might think I have something of theirs and they might want it back."

Maggie's skin prickled. "Something? Like what?" Could he be in the same situation as her? Only Charlie didn't have a baby for the Sukas to kidnap and use as collateral for a trade.

"I can't say." For the first time since he'd come into her house, he looked around at the scattered cushions and items littering the floor. "What happened here?"

Maggie let the blinds go. "Someone broke in last night while I was out looking for Dakota."

Charlie's brows furrowed. "I heard about that. I guess they haven't found him yet?"

"No. Someone snatched him out of his bed early yesterday morning." She almost choked on the words, the memory of waking to find her son gone almost knocking her to her knees. Would the nightmare ever fade? Probably not until her son came home.

"I'm sorry." He patted her shoulder in an awkward teenaged-boy manner. "I have a baby sister. I'd kill anyone who hurt her." Big words for such a young man.

Though she didn't believe in killing another human, the thought had crossed her mind. For a moment, she fought the rush of rage filling up the empty parts in her soul. If Maggie could get her hands on whoever had Dakota, she'd come as close to murder as she'd ever contemplated in her entire life. "They're holding him for ransom."

The boy's brown eyes narrowed and he stared around at her simple house, filled with worn furniture. "What do they want?"

"That's just it. I don't know. They say they want what was stolen. But I haven't stolen anything that I know of." She glanced across at Charlie as a thought ran through her mind. "You don't know what they might be talking about, do you?"

"No." He backed up a step, shaking his head a little too hard. "I don't know what they're talking about. Any idea who they are?"

"No, just a call on my telephone with the offer to trade what was stolen for my son."

"Damn." His gaze fell to his feet. "I shouldn't have come," he said for the second time.

She crossed her arms over her chest, too tired to play word games with the boy. "Why did you come?"

"I needed someone to talk to. But I don't want to bother you." He edged toward the door. "You have your own problems."

"Charlie Tatanka," Maggie's fingers dug into his arm. "If you know anything, anything at all, you have to tell me."

He shrugged her hand off and stepped around her. "I have to go."

"Wait, Charlie!" She reached the door before he did and took a deep calming breath. Scaring the kid wouldn't get him to talk. "You're already here. You might as well tell me why you came. I promise to listen."

"It doesn't matter. It's my mess, and I have to get out of it myself."

"What if I can help?" she offered. The boy was scared, and he was hiding something. Maggie wanted to stomp her foot in frustration. But no amount of stomping would make him open up if he didn't want to.

"You can't help." Charlie stared into her eyes. "No one can. I have to do this myself."

He couldn't leave, not when he might know something that could help her find her son. "Please, Charlie," Maggie said, her voice a mere whisper.

For a moment, Charlie hesitated as if he wanted to tell her something, but in the end, he stood in front of her. "I need to go. I shouldn't have come."

He reached around her and opened the door.

Maggie was forced to move or be moved. She stepped aside and watched as Charlie glanced out, and then slipped through the door and around the back of the house, gone as though he'd never been there, taking with him some knowledge that might have helped her save her son.

JOE'S THOUGHTS tumbled through his head on the drive to the murder scene. He'd lain awake until three that morning, his mind replaying what Maggie had told him as she drifted off to sleep.

She'd done as he'd expected.

He'd told her she didn't have a place in his life as a Lakota Indian. Did that mean she'd married his white stepbrother because he, Joe Lonewolf, expected it?

What the hell did she mean by that? Short of shaking her awake and asking her, he didn't have a clue. Could the tough but gentle Maggie really have married his stepbrother to spite him? Did that mean she'd never loved Paul? Joe shook his head. Maggie didn't have a spiteful bone in her body.

After stewing for hours over her statement, Joe had drifted

off into a restless sleep, plagued with nightmares of a crying baby, a smoky sweat lodge and a message from Matoskah.

What did it all mean? Were his dreams supposed to help him in his search to find Dakota? Joe wanted to swing by Matoskah's house and ask, but he didn't have time. One of his tribe was dead and another in the hospital. He had a job to do.

Alternating between being pissed off and totally confused, Joe accomplished the drive across seven miles of town and prairie, coming up with more questions than answers.

He pulled his SUV to the side of the road behind the ambulance waiting to take Bernie Two Eagle's body to the reservation morgue. Delaney Toke stood next to the FBI agent, Chase Metcalf, talking quietly, while special agents of the South Dakota Division of Criminal Investigation (DCI) snapped pictures of the scene and collected evidence in plastic bags.

Bernie lay on the slope of the roadside ditch, a white-handled antique revolver lying in the dead brown grass next to his right hand.

From where Joe stood, he could see where the bullet had entered Bernie's temple. He had no desire to see where the bullet had exited on the other side, but he needed to know. He needed to know for certain whether this was a case of suicide or murder.

Having been to Iraq and bearing witness to terrorist atrocities first-hand, he still couldn't help the natural gag reflex when he circled Bernie and stared at what wasn't remaining of the left side of the Native American's head.

"Had breakfast, Joe?" Del patted his back.

"No. Thank goodness."

"Yeah. I left mine over there." Del jerked his head toward a spot several yards away.

Chase Metcalf joined them.

"You do this all the time, Metcalf," Del said. "Do you ever get used to seeing this kinda thing?"

"No." Agent Metcalf said in a clipped voice.

"Then how do you do it?" Del's reddish-brown skin had a sallow tint. "How do you turn it off?"

Chase shrugged. "You just do, or you'd never get out of bed in the morning and never eat another meal."

Joe heard Del and Chase, but their words were nothing more than white noise. "Bernie was my father's friend."

Del nodded. "Everyone on the reservation liked him."

"From the angle of the exit wound, I'd say this wasn't suicide."

"No. It wasn't."

"How can you be so sure?" Metcalf asked.

"Bernie was left-handed. If it was suicide, the gun would have been in his left hand, not the right." Joe looked out across the plains, scratching his brain for answers and coming up blank. "Who would want to murder an old man?"

"The same person who tried to kill Tom Little Elk last night," Chase responded.

"What do the two have in common other than they live on the same reservation?" Joe mused aloud. "They weren't particularly close." Something about the pistol triggered a shadow of a memory. Joe leaned closer. "Del? Did you see this?"

"See what?" He moved up beside Joe.

"The pistol," Joe said. "I *know* that pistol."

Metcalf squatted next to the gun. "Looks old, like an antique."

Joe knew this gun. He'd seen it a hundred times. "I'd bet next month's salary it's a Colt .45 single-action army pistol made in 1857 and given to—"

"—George Tatanka's great-great-grandfather by Chief Thunder Hawk," Del finished, shaking his head.

George had spoken the same words each year at the annual Painted Rock Lakota Powwow, while holding the infamous pistol out in front of him like a sacred idol.

Joe resisted reaching out for the prized possession of one of his people. "What the hell's it doing here?"

Dell straightened. "Let's go ask George."

"Question his kid while you're at it." One of the DCI special agents lifted a tattered baseball cap with Painted Road Warriors written across the front in faded red letters. "Found it under the body."

Chapter Seven

As she walked down the shiny, waxed corridors of the Painted Rock Reservation Hospital, the scent of alcohol and disinfectant cleaners stung Maggie's nostrils. The last time she'd been in this hospital had been to deliver her son. Her chest tightened and her feet faltered. How could such a small child who'd been on this earth only a short time make his way so firmly into her heart?

Dakota was her son and part of Joe. The only part of Joe she could ever have.

Paul had tried to edge his way into her heart. When she'd gone into labor, he'd been there to drive her to the hospital, and he would have stood by her throughout the delivery, had she let him.

If not for the constant attention from the nurses, Maggie would have been alone with her regret: she regretted imposing a sham marriage on Paul, regretted that halfway around the world, the baby's father was fighting a hopeless war against terrorists and was completely unaware of the impending arrival of his son.

Now, guilt still squeezed at her heart. She should have told

Joe about Dakota as soon as she'd known she was pregnant. She'd been wrong to keep the knowledge from him.

Resolving to tell him as soon as the opportunity presented itself, Maggie showed her driver's license to the police officer stationed in the hallway and then opened the door to Room 18.

"Winona?" she called out softly. A vinyl chair squeaked and the older woman appeared beside the curtain drawn around the high bed. Her usually happy face was pensive, her big brown eyes puffy and bloodshot.

Maggie went to the woman and wrapped her in her arms. "I'm so sorry."

"He's a strong man. He'll recover," Winona said, pulling away to dab at the tears in her eyes. Her glance strayed to the man on the bed. "I don't know what I'd do without my Tom." She drifted back to the bed and lifted the one hand that was free of tubes and needles. "He wouldn't hurt anyone. Why would someone want to kill him?"

"I don't know, Winona." Maggie stared out the window onto the cold, gray day. Her heart ached from worry. "Why would someone want to take a baby away from his mother?" A tear slipped unbidden down her cheek and she dashed it away. "Has Tom talked to you since they brought him in?"

"No. Someone shot at him while he was driving home from work last night. When a bullet hit him in the shoulder, he skidded off the road and the car hit a telephone pole. He's been out since they found him." Winona sniffed and squeezed Tom's hand. "I love him so much I don't think I could live without him."

Moisture pooled in Maggie's eyes, but she fought back

further tears and the envy she felt for the love Winona had for Tom. Would she ever find that kind of love?

Yes. She already had.

She loved Joe that much, but he didn't love her as Tom loved his Winona. Maggie had seen them together when she'd picked up Dakota after work. Tom and Winona had a comfortable yet playful relationship, acting like kids at times. But their love was obvious for everyone to see, a testament to time and a long life together.

Maggie turned to the window so that she wouldn't have to see what she was missing. Her life was complete with Dakota. What more could a woman ask for than to raise her son?

The love of a man. The words whispered in the back of her consciousness.

A soft snort escaped her. Perhaps she was asking too much of life. Right now, she'd settle for getting her son back. Maybe she would reevaluate her life on the reservation and go back to Des Moines and the city life. The reservation wasn't big enough for both Joe and her. She couldn't stand to bump into him all the time, knowing he could never love her.

But then there was Dakota to think of. If she left, Joe wouldn't have access to his son. Or worse, the tribe might choose to sue for custody of Dakota to have him raised as an American Indian.

Her son. The baby boy she'd grown to love more than life itself.

Maggie wanted to throw open the window and shout to the world, "Where is my son?" She leaned her forehead against the glass to cool her rising anger. Anger and despair weren't helping her to find her son or Bernie's killer. She straightened away from the window. "Winona, is there anything I can do for you?"

"No," Winona said, pressing Tom's hand to her wrinkled cheek. "I'm just going to hang out here until Tom wakes."

"I'll be back later to check on you two. Call me on my cell if you want me to bring you anything."

"Thank you, Maggie." She didn't walk with Maggie to the door, choosing to stay by her husband's bedside.

Easing the door closed, Maggie walked down the long hall toward the exit, her pace quickening as she went until her footfalls echoed loudly against the walls.

She'd find her son if it was the last thing she did. And Joe Lonewolf was the man to help her. As the boy's father, he had a right to know Dakota was his son.

Maggie didn't quite remember how she accomplished the short drive from the hospital to the tribal police station. Her mind was already there, trying to figure out a way to get Joe alone so she could tell him what he needed to know.

She pulled into the parking lot at the same time as one of the black SUVs the tribal police used. She held her breath, hoping Joe would get out, but was disappointed when Delaney Toke climbed down and waved.

After parking in a space further along the line of vehicles, Maggie grabbed her purse, bolstered her courage and unfolded herself from her compact car.

Delaney held open the back door of his SUV and a man who was vaguely familiar climbed out. The man was followed by a scared teen dressed in a camouflage army jacket Maggie recognized.

Charlie Tatanka.

JOE'S HEAD hurt from his visit to Bernie Two Eagles's wife to tell her the sad news of her husband's death. He'd rather lose his right arm than tell another woman a loved one had died. Tillie Two Eagles had stood there in silence for the first full five seconds, her dark brows coming together over her nose as if she didn't quite understand what he'd said. "My Bernie's dead? But he was just at the casino last night. I thought he'd stayed until morning because he was winning. He does that, you know."

"Yes, ma'am," Joe had said holding his hat in his hands. "I'm sorry, Mrs. Two Eagles."

Her face crumpled into a pathetic, lost look. "But how?"

His next words were almost as hard as the first announcement. "Gunshot wounds."

"Gunshot?" Her voice wavered, her eyes filling with tears and then she sank to the floor in a sobbing heap.

Joe was sure her wails could be heard from one end of the reservation to the other. He'd wished he'd brought along one of the women from the station. Over the next fifteen minutes, he settled Mrs. Two Eagles on her couch and called for her grown daughter, Laney, to come immediately. Once Laney arrived, he delivered the same message and then made a hasty getaway, glad to be away from so many exposed emotions.

Bernie had been his father's friend, but the man's death didn't call forth tears from Joe Lonewolf. No sir. It filled him with anger at the injustice. Joe wanted Bernie's killer and he damned well would get him.

Having done his civic duty toward Mrs. Two Eagles and her daughter, Joe hurried back to the station to get on with the investigation, making a quick call to the team of officers canvassing the isolated pockets of housing scattered across the reservation. Nothing yet. No sign of a red-haired baby.

While he was on the phone trying to locate Gray Running Fox, the manager of the casino, George and Charlie Tatanka were ushered in. Maggie Brandt followed close behind.

He squeezed the bridge of his nose to stem the rising headache. Something had to break in this case, and it had better not be him. He rose from his chair and met George halfway across the floor crowded with desks and people. "George."

"Joe." George held out his hand and Joe shook it. "I didn't shoot Bernie Two Eagles. You gotta believe me."

Del stood beside George. "When I asked him about the gun, he thought it was still in his house. Even went to the gun cabinet to show me." The younger officer shrugged. "It wasn't there and the lock hadn't been forced or anything."

"Did you dust for prints?" Joe asked.

Del nodded. "Sure did."

"I don't know how that gun got out of my house without me knowing about it. But I didn't shoot Bernie and neither did Charlie." He hooked an arm around his son's shoulders. "Tell 'em, Charlie."

"I didn't kill nobody," Charlie said, his chin low and his eyes shifting from left to right like those of a trapped animal.

"How do you explain the hat we found next to his body?" Delaney said, holding up the evidence bag containing the Warriors hat.

"That's my hat!" Charlie reached out to grab the bag, but Del jerked it out of his reach.

"Sorry. You won't be getting it back anytime soon," Del said. "It's evidence now."

"It's been missing for a week now. I looked everywhere, didn't I, Dad?" Charlie's eyes narrowed. "Someone's setting me up."

Joe didn't for a minute believe either Charlie or George had shot Bernie, but something in the way the kid was acting sparked warning flares in Joe's mind. "And who would try to set you up?"

"I—" Charlie's brown gaze shot around the room full of adults until it landed on Maggie's face. For a brief second he looked like he wanted to run and hide, but the moment was so short, Joe thought he might have imagined it. "I don't know."

"Don't know? Or won't tell?" Del crossed his arms over his chest and stood tall, his six-foot frame towering over the boy who was a good head shorter than himself.

"I don't have to tell you anything," Charlie said. "I have rights."

"And what rights are those?" George Tatanka eyed his son down the bridge of his nose, the same look his ancestors had used when facing down enemies in a fierce battle. "If you know something, you'd better tell the officers."

Charlie dug his hands into his pockets and stared at the floor. "I don't know anything."

"Look—" Del stepped closer.

Joe moved between Delaney and Charlie. "Why don't you check in at the hospital and see if Tom Little Elk has regained consciousness yet."

"Why don't I just call?" Del asked.

"I want you to go there. If he has anything to say, I want

you to be the one to hear it," Joe said, his voice firm. It was the same don't-mess-with-me tone he'd used with his young troops in Iraq.

"Right, boss. I'll be back shortly." Del shot a last look at Charlie and George. "Are you sure you don't need me here?"

Joe nodded. "I'm sure." After Del left, Joe handed George over to agent Metcalf for questioning on the stolen gun and then he turned to Charlie and Maggie. "Come on."

"What do you mean?" Maggie asked.

"You two are coming with me," he said and turned to walk away.

"Where?" Charlie asked, his gaze tracking his father as he followed the FBI agent to an empty desk in the corner. "Is my dad going to be all right?"

"As long as he didn't kill Bernie Two Eagles," Joe said.

"He didn't kill Bernie!" Charlie's vehement response came out as a harsh whisper in the busy station.

Joe didn't relent. He wanted Charlie scared. Scared teens tended to talk. "It was his gun."

"Someone stole it."

"Like I said, follow me." Joe walked away, and Charlie followed.

"You gonna lock me up?" Charlie asked as Joe led him through the maze of hallways to the garage on the other side of the long building.

"You can't lock him up, Joe. He didn't kill Bernie," Maggie said, trotting to keep up.

"Are you sure?" he asked. "Were you there?"

A frown creased her forehead. "No, but a person's innocent until proven guilty. I know that much about the law."

"Things are a little different on the reservation than they

are on the outside. Aren't they Charlie?" Joe paused in front of a heavy metal door and turned to face Charlie and Maggie.

"Not that much different." The teen scuffed his shoe in front of him, his chin tucked against his chest. The frown he gave Joe was fierce enough to burn him in Hell.

"Here on the reservation, we like to duke it out."

"Huh?" Maggie asked. "You can't fight Charlie, he's just a kid."

"What she said," Charlie backed away. "You must weigh twice as much as I do."

Joe flung the door open to the old station garage they'd converted into a combination workout room and basketball court. "One-on-one," he said. "Or in this case, one-on-two. You and Mrs. Brandt against me. If I win, you have to tell me what you know. If you win, you can go away without spilling a word."

Charlie frowned at Maggie as he shed his camouflage jacket. "She can't play."

"Okay, I'll take her as my handicap."

"Thanks." Maggie's voice was flat and her lips twisted into a cross between a smile and a frown. On anyone else, the look would be considered a grimace. On Maggie, with her wild red hair and freckles sprinkled across her nose, it was cute.

Joe squashed the urge to kiss her. Whatever Charlie wasn't saying might play into finding Bernie's killer and Maggie's baby. He lifted a basketball from the trash can full of balls in the corner and tossed it to Charlie. "First one to reach seven wins. Go."

Charlie scowled and he pivoted to the left, leaving Joe standing next to Maggie. The ball left his hand, bounced off the backboard and landed in the hoop.

"Two zero, your ball." Charlie tossed the ball to Joe and rolled his eyes. "At this rate, I'll have seven in fewer than five minutes."

"Cocky, isn't he?" Joe shoved the ball into Maggie's hands and sprinted across the floor.

He'd shown her a few moves back before he left for Iraq, and he just hoped she remembered. Maggie dribbled twice, her eyes wide with what looked like panic. Then she threw the ball over Charlie's head right into Joe's hands.

"Good girl." He lobbed the ball into the hoop. "Nothin' but air. Two up, buddy." He shoved the ball into Charlie's hands and the boy was all over the court, dodging Maggie easily but finding it a little more difficult to dart around Joe.

Everywhere Charlie turned, Joe was there. He sensed the boy's frustration and let up a little. Enough to make the teen feel like he had a break. Then he closed in and stole the ball from Charlie and shot another basket.

"Four to two," Maggie said, standing on the sidelines now, out of the way of the two playing.

Charlie scored the next four points and Maggie's face looked strained. But Joe wasn't worried. He knew how Charlie worked by now and the directions he liked to go. When the teen dodged left, Joe compensated and stole the ball from him, landing a three-point shot from center court.

"Five to six," Charlie said, a bead of sweat trickling down the side of his face. "Next score wins."

"Give up?" Joe asked.

Charlie shook his head and Joe thrust the ball into his chest.

A little slower on his feet than when he was sixteen, Joe was glad he'd had time to shoot a few hoops and keep up with his physical fitness while stationed in Baghdad. For a thirty-one-year-old man wearing boots and a uniform, he was holding his own, but he didn't have the stamina of a teen.

Charlie almost made it around him while he was patting himself on the back for being in shape and the strained look on Maggie's face was getting to him. Tired and ready to end the challenge, Joe seized the ball and scored the last points of the game.

Breathing hard and a little sweaty, he approached Charlie with his hand held out to shake. "Good game."

Charlie took his hand, but refused to meet his gaze. Now that the time had come to fess up, he didn't look like he'd live up to his end of the bargain.

But Joe was mistaken when Charlie looked up. "I stole something from the Sukas."

"What?" Maggie stepped up to the man and boy in the middle of the court.

The teen's gaze shifted from Joe back to Maggie. "A stash of ice."

"Meth? The same stuff Kiya overdosed on?" Maggie asked.

"Yeah." His eyes widened, and he held his hand out to Maggie. "Kiya was my friend and she was clean the last time I saw her…alive." He bent his head. "I didn't want anybody else to die and this was the only way I could think of helping."

"How much did you steal?" Joe asked.

"Maybe two pounds, from what I could tell."

"Damn," Joe muttered.

Maggie laid a hand on Charlie's arm. "Where is it?"

"I hid it in the center."

Her hand rose to cover her mouth, her eyes wide. "And the Sukas think you took it? Do they think I helped?" Had Charlie's attempt to save other kids from a death like Kiya's backfired and drawn her and Dakota into the mess?

"I didn't think they saw me. I did it in the middle of the night when no one was around the house."

"Wait a minute, Charlie." Joe raised a hand. "What house? Where?"

"That abandoned shack near Rock City. The Sukas have been known to hang out there. They call it the Den. Now they'll kill me for telling anyone. I'm in so much trouble. I just wanted to save some other kids from dying like Kiya." Charlie turned and walked a few steps away before he pivoted in his tennis shoes and faced Maggie. "But if they stole your kid to get the stash back, you can have it."

"Oh my God, Joe. Do you think those kids took Dakota?" She touched a hand to his arm, hope welling in her eyes only for a moment before her gaze turned to a worried frown. "How could they possibly take care of a baby for three days? Those kids haven't had that kind of responsibility. They'll get impatient and tired of hearing him cry. We have to find him." She grabbed Joe's arm and pulled him toward the door. "Come on."

"Not so fast." Joe slipped an arm around Maggie's waist and held her still before turning back to Charlie. "When did you take the drugs?"

"Last night."

Joe shook his head. "Dakota disappeared two nights ago. I'm not convinced they knew about Maggie's involvement before the child disappeared."

"But Joe, this is the only lead we have!" Maggie tried to pry his fingers from her waist, but he held tight.

"We'll check into it and question the Sukas, but I don't want you anywhere near their hangout." He turned her to face him. "Do you understand me? You're not to go there."

"But they could have Dakota." She had to go out there, had to know.

"And then again, they might not. And if you invade their territory, they might decide you're fair game. Leave it to the investigation team."

"But—"

"No buts." Joe grabbed Charlie's camouflage army jacket from where he'd dropped it on the floor and tossed it to him. "Come on, Charlie. I want you to show us where this stash is."

Chapter Eight

Charlie led them to the center and inside to the janitorial supply closet. Buried deep beneath a pile of old rags was a plastic bag packed tightly with crystallized white powder.

Methamphetamines, otherwise known on the streets as meth, crystal or ice. One of the scariest homemade drugs in America. Maggie knew just how lethal this drug was. She'd done her homework, and she'd seen Kiya in rehab going through a very painful detoxification. This poison was even more addictive than cocaine, and this quantity was a large amount for kids to be hiding.

"I've got Delaney and another squad car on their way out to the Den to see what else they can find. I'm betting they won't find anything."

"You should have let me go too." Anger still burned in the back of her throat. She should be out there too, not forced to stay in town where it was supposedly safe.

Her son had been stolen from his bed in this "safe" town. Maggie fought the tears building behind her eyelids.

Joe held the bag out. "Think about it, Maggie. If they know Charlie has this stuff, they'll also know that he knew where to find it. They will have cleared the building of any further evidence."

Maggie chewed on her lip. "You're probably right," she admitted. "But I don't have to like it." If there were any possibility Dakota was hidden in the Den, she wanted to be there for him, but Joe's words made too much sense, darn it.

In a softer tone, he added, "The exchange meeting is for tomorrow night. If the meth stash is what they want for Dakota, you can take it."

"I can?" She wasn't sure she wanted to be responsible for all that meth. Hell, she didn't even want to touch it. But, if it meant her son's life, she'd give it to them.

"Well, something that looks just like it, anyway." Joe glanced down at the tightly wrapped bag. "I'm still not sure that this is what the kidnappers are after. I'm not even sure the Sukas are responsible for Dakota's disappearance."

Frustration bubbled up inside and Maggie quelled the urge to reach out and shake Joe. "What makes you think that? The drugs are the only stolen items I know of, unless you have other evidence you're not telling me about?"

"No." He shrugged. "Call it gut feel."

"Well, gut feel isn't getting my son back. We have to have more to go on than that. In the meantime, what'll happen to Charlie?"

"You gonna charge me with possession?" Charlie asked, his expression a cross between stubborn teen and scared kid.

"No, Charlie. By pulling this stuff off the streets, you've done a service to the youth on the reservation." Joe rested his free hand on the boy's shoulder. "But don't do it again.

You could have gotten yourself killed. Next time you know something, bring it straight to me."

"There won't be a next time. Those guys will never trust me again." He shrugged. "I'm thinking its time to move in with my mother and stepfather in Rapid City."

"Oh, Charlie." Maggie grabbed his hands and squeezed them, letting go a moment later when she realized she was probably embarrassing him. "I'd hate to think of you leaving the reservation. You've always been a friend and a great help to me."

"Maybe," he said, his cheeks reddening. "But these guys play for keeps. A snitch doesn't last long around here."

"We'll take care of the Sukas, Charlie." Joe's eyes hardened. "Is Randy Biko still the leader?"

"Yeah, only they call him Snake now. And he was Kiya's boyfriend." The teen snorted. "Some boyfriend. If she'd been *my* girlfriend, I wouldn't have given her the drugs." He almost choked on the last word.

"You and Kiya were close, weren't you?" Maggie slipped an arm around Charlie's shoulder.

The muscles in his throat constricted. First one, then another tear trailed down his dark-skinned cheeks. "I would have taken care of her."

Maggie swallowed hard, her eyes burning. "I know. You were a good friend, Charlie. Kiya would have been proud of what you did."

"Wish I'd done it before—" His words choked off and he gulped.

"I know. I miss her, too." Maggie pulled him into her arms and hugged him as the tears flowed silently down his face. She stared over his shoulder to Joe standing silently, a frown wrinkling his smooth forehead and his dark eyes glistening in the dim lighting of the garage.

He cared about the kids on the reservation as much as she did. That was one of the reasons she'd fallen for him. Sometimes people like her and Joe cared too much, putting their own lives into danger. What was worse was when they put the lives of those people they loved most in the same danger. Like her innocent child.

When Charlie pulled away, he swiped at his eyes with the sleeve of his black-and-green jacket. "I better check on my dad." His gaze captured Joe's and he held it for a long moment. "He didn't kill Bernie, Officer Lonewolf. I know my dad. He wouldn't kill anyone."

Joe nodded without affirming or denying, as if he accepted the word of the teenager in lieu of due process.

Since Maggie had known Charlie, he'd never lied to her. And as far as she could tell, George Tatanka didn't have an obvious motivation to kill Bernie.

"Have you seen anyone hanging around your house lately?" Maggie asked.

"No. But then neither one of us has been around much. I got a part-time job down at the truck stop bussing tables after school and my dad works two jobs just to make enough for us to live."

Maggie knew how hard Charlie and his father worked for what they got. They didn't believe in taking handouts from the government, not when they were strong and able-bodied. They were Lakota, independent and proud of it.

She wished more of the kids were as smart and focused as Charlie. He'd make something of himself someday. If he didn't get himself killed.

JOE LEFT Maggie and Charlie with Agent Metcalf to document Charlie's statement. George Tatanka stood by, nursing a paper cup of coffee, just as shocked and concerned about the drugs, gun theft and killing as the tribal police.

The baby's disappearance, Tom's and Bernie's shooting incidents and the stolen drugs had all occurred in the past couple of days. Joe struggled to make the connection between what appeared to be three isolated actions.

From Tillie Two Eagles's account, Bernie had been out at the Grand Buffalo Casino last night. Tom worked nights there as a janitor. He might be chasing a false lead, but Joe felt compelled to drive out to the casino and sniff around, maybe ask a few questions.

The twenty-minute drive gave him too much time to mull over the evidence with enough time left over to think about Maggie. Hell, she was clouding every thought in his head.

He was almost relieved to see the gaudy casino perched on the prairie, its neon lights shining despite the fact it was daytime. At least by doing his job, he could set thoughts of the pretty social worker out of his mind.

When he pulled to a stop, Joe stared through his windshield and shook his head, saddened by the garish sight. A brick-and-mortar monolith of architecture sat in the middle of a wide expanse of pavement, topped by the words *Grand Buffalo Casino* flashing in six-foot-high red neon letters. The complex clashed with the dried prairie grasses where buffalo had roamed in the not-too-distant past.

As soon as he stepped through the brass-handled doors of the Grand Buffalo Casino, he was assailed by the stench of cigarette smoke. Daytime was the only time the casino wasn't packed to the hilt with a crowd bent on losing their money in a hurry. By five o'clock in the afternoon, the place would start filling. People left work and came in for an evening's entertainment, punching buttons on the slot machines or watching the roulette wheels spin until they stopped. Upstanding reservation citizens like Bernie Two Eagles, who'd never had a problem saving money until the casino came to the reservation, couldn't resist the draw. Even good people could be led astray when it came to the vice of gambling.

Joe had never wanted the casino on the reservation, but the money it brought in had helped the tribe build new schools and the reservation hospital, so he tolerated its presence and tried to keep the peace in and around it. But he couldn't tell people how to spend their money.

Crossing the colorful, Vegas-style carpets, Joe nodded to the Native American employees he recognized, and made his way toward the back of the casino where the offices were located. The brassy musical sounds of the various gambling machines and the clinking of coins dropping one at a time into the metal trays surrounded him, making his head pound.

"Hi, stranger." A low, sexy voice sounded in his ear and brightly painted fingernails crawled over his shoulder.

"Leotie." He lifted her hand off his shirt and placed it by her side. The dark-haired woman was too obvious and tiring. One of Joe's main regrets in his life was sleeping with Leotie Jones when they were barely out of their teens and still trying to "find themselves" on the reservation. Since then, she'd made it her life's mission to remind him of it. Her pursuit had been relentless to the point of obsessive. She'd even tried to run him off the road once to get his attention, although she'd said she didn't see him.

After a decade of telling her he wasn't interested, Joe would have thought she'd get the message.

Leotie might not be able to take a hint, but she was very persistent and she had a mean streak the size of South Dakota. "Heard about Bernie Two Eagles. Such a shame." She was haughty, brazen and anything but regretful. "Saw him here last night. The way he was losing at the slots, I'm not surprised he committed suicide."

"Who said he committed suicide?" Joe stared hard at her until her eyelids flickered and dropped over her deep-brown eyes. She twirled a strand of her red-tinted black hair, her eyes narrowing to charcoal-lined slits.

"Isn't that why you're out here?" she asked.

"Could be."

"You only come out here when there's trouble." Her lips thinned and she pinned him with her gaze. "Now that Paul's dead, you and that social worker a thing again?" It was just like Leotie to get right to what was eating at her. She had always been jealous of his relationship with Maggie, or rather his former relationship.

"Don't go there, Leotie." Joe held his temper in check. He and Paul hadn't been close—a fact Joe regretted more each day—but Leotie had no right to infer Joe was glad Paul was out of the way so that he could pursue his step-brother's widow. "What I do in my private life is none of your business. Now, if you'll excuse me, I'm here on official business."

She shrugged and moved aside.

As he passed, she smirked. "Did you know that your

pretty little social worker has her own secrets to hide? I wouldn't trust her if I were you. Not all is as it appears on the surface."

She's just trying to get a rise out of you. Don't react. Joe took two steps, but despite his internal warning, he couldn't help turning back toward Leotie.

As he'd expected, she had the self-satisfied smile of the cat that had swallowed the pet hamster.

He knew he was wasting his time, but Joe marched up to Leotie. "Maggie Brandt is something you aren't. She's nice. She cares about other people, and she doesn't have a dishonest bone in her body." He raised his brow as if waiting for her to challenge his statement.

She snorted but didn't say a word while he was in her face.

And a good thing, too. Joe wasn't certain how much control he had on his anger at the moment. "Stay away from her and stay away from me," were his parting words. His heels dug into the carpeted floor as he set off for the offices.

Before he got more than a yard, Leotie's voice brought him to a halt—she always did have to get in the last word.

"At least you *know* I'm dishonest. But you were always blind where Maggie was concerned," she said. "Did you bother to ask her why she married Paul?"

He didn't respond, just kept walking, Leotie's coarse laughter grating against his ears.

The woman liked stirring up trouble, even back in high school she'd played her friends against each other, earning a bad reputation with the girls. She wasn't above getting physical, and not just in the sexual sense. In her sophomore year, she'd started a fistfight with Stewart Strong Bow for bumping into her in the hallway.

Stewart had ended up in the hospital with ten stitches over his right eye, and Leotie had earned the status of being dangerous. No one wanted to cross her after that incident.

Since Joe showed an interest in Maggie, Leotie'd had it out for her. Maybe he should warn Maggie to watch out for one of her pranks.

He slowed, remembering the rock through the window last night. Could that have been Leotie in a fit of anger?

"Joe Lonewolf. What brings you to our neck of the woods?" Gray Running Fox stepped through the doorway leading into the administrative offices. He was followed by a distinguished looking white-haired man Joe recognized as the regional representative from the National Indian Gaming Commission. Joe had seen him during the tribal meetings at the onset of the casino development project.

The man was in his well-preserved mid-fifties, his white hair the only concession to age. Both he and Gray wore black suits, crisp white shirts and red power ties as if it were the uniform of the day for casino management. If Joe wasn't already irritated by the Leotie encounter, he'd laugh.

"I wouldn't call a casino the woods," Joe said, staring at the packed rows of brightly lit slot machines making their annoying dinging sounds.

"Maybe not, but around here money grows on trees. Right, Mr. Caldwell?" Gray laughed.

It sounded forced to Joe, yet Gray didn't look in the least uncomfortable. Why should his laugh sound forced?

The white-haired gentleman didn't even crack a smile. He gave Gray a pointed look, his eyes narrowing slightly. "I'll check back with you later."

"You bet. Have a safe drive back to Rapid City." Gray held out his hand for Mr. Caldwell to shake.

The older man ignored it and without another word and only a brief nod in Joe's direction, he walked away.

"Not very talkative, is he?" Joe asked.

"Who?" Gray smiled. "Mr. Caldwell?"

Joe resisted responding to the sarcasm evident in Gray's words and asked instead, "Everything okay with the casino?"

"Absolutely. Couldn't be better." His words sounded cheerful and confident, but his gaze followed the older man across the casino floor until he exited the front door. Then he turned his attention to Joe. "What can I do for you?"

"You know Bernie Two Eagles was found in a ditch this morning with a bullet through his head, don't you?"

Gray's forehead creased. "Yeah, I'd heard. Also heard about Tom."

Joe thought as much. Good and bad news traveled quickly within the tribe.

Gray's frown deepened. "What does it have to do with the casino?"

"Bernie's wife said he was out here last night. I'm back-tracking to see if I can come up with a reason."

"I heard it was suicide," Gray said.

"That's what it looked like." Joe didn't bother to correct Gray. Until he understood a little more about the case, he wasn't advertising the fact Bernie was murdered.

"The staff from last night comes on duty in thirty minutes. You're welcome to hang around until then. In the meantime, are there any questions I can answer for you?"

"Were you here last night at the same time as Bernie and Tom?"

"I wasn't working last night, at least not here," Gray said. "I had dinner with Mr. Caldwell at the Crazy Horse Steak House."

Joe was familiar with the place. It was the only decent restaurant in the small town of Broken Elbow, just outside the Painted Rock Reservation. "So you weren't here at all last night?"

"Only long enough to drop Mr. Caldwell off at his car before I headed home."

Joe had seen Gray's home. It sat on one of the many rolling hills of native prairie grass, the stone columns and stucco walls incongruous with the modest and sometimes ramshackle homes of other Lakotans. "You must be doing well as the manager of the Grand Buffalo."

"I can't lie. The money's good. We're proud of the fact we've kept the management within the tribe unlike some reservations that hire out the administration of their casinos to outside organizations. At Painted Rock we've kept ours in the tribe." His chest swelled bigger with each word that sounded more like an advertisement than conversation.

"We figured you'd end up in sales or management one day. You always could talk a great line of bull." Joe smiled to soften the dig. They'd been friends in high school, cracking jokes and taking punches at each other. But that had been a long time ago.

"Me, too. Only, when we were growing up, I never pictured this." Gray's gaze panned the room, his lips curling upward. "In fact, I never pictured myself coming back to Painted Rock after high school."

"Yeah, I thought you said you'd never come back. Especially once you hit Vegas." Joe shook his head. He'd never understood how Gray could prefer the crowds and traffic of a busy resort city over the big skies and close friendships of the tribe and the reservation life. But then Gray had always walked in his own path.

"I learned a lot about casino management at the Lucky You Casino in Vegas, and I probably would have stayed."

"So you came back for the job?"

"Mr. Caldwell made me an offer I couldn't refuse. I had to come back." He said the words in a matter-of-fact tone.

Joe had been thrilled to come back from the war in Iraq. Painted Rock was his home. Although life was hard on the reservation, he loved his people, their way of life and the wisdom of his ancestors. "Didn't you want to come back?"

Gray shrugged. "Don't get me wrong. This will always be home, but I loved the excitement and energy of Vegas. There was always something going on at all hours." He nodded a greeting to an employee walking by.

"Have you had any problems here?" Joe asked.

"Just trying to find a replacement for Paul." His gaze met Joe's. "Sorry. Sometimes I forget you two were brothers."

In the past, Joe would have corrected Gray by interjecting stepbrother. Not today. Paul's death was too fresh on his mind and the regrets he felt too real to ignore. "What did Paul do around here?" Besides the fact Paul had married Maggie, Joe didn't know much about his brother's life.

"He was our computer guru. He designed databases for everything from the work schedule to employee information. When Murray needed help storing the accounting data, Paul designed a database for that. He was amazing with a computer."

Paul had always had an affinity for electronics. He'd

gotten a part-time job while going to high school just to earn money for his own system. When he'd graduated, he'd attended the community college. Joe was amazed at how much Paul had learned on his own. Joe knew his way around installing prepackaged software, but nothing whatsoever about creating his own.

"We were all devastated by Paul's loss." Gray laid an arm around Joe's shoulder. "And he loved Maggie, although I don't know what was happening on the home front. He never talked about it, just started spending more and more time at work." Gray shrugged. "He'd have done anything for her."

Those words ate a hole straight through Joe's stomach. Paul loved Maggie and would have done anything for her, whereas Joe had turned away from her. No. Joe had flat-out dumped her. He'd been a jerk and he hadn't deserved Maggie. Not until he was halfway around the world and ducking bullets with his soldier brothers had he realized the error of his ways.

"There's Murray now," Gray said. "He was here until midnight last night. Maybe he knows something about Bernie."

Joe turned toward the man with the light-gray pinstripe suit hanging loosely on his narrow frame. "I don't think we've met. I'm Joe Lonewolf, chief of tribal police."

"No, we haven't met. I came on shortly after your unit left for the war." Murray was a skinny little man with granny glasses and a pinched face. He carried his briefcase across his chest like a shield, lowering it enough to place his pale, white hand in Joe's.

Joe almost jerked his hand back. Shaking hands with

Murray was like shaking a dead fish. His hand was limp, cool and clammy.

Murray pulled his hand away quickly, bracing it around his case again as if it took two hands to hold the thin satchel.

Okay, so Murray wasn't a tough guy. He must make up for it with his brain. Joe hoped so. He'd never have survived on his own on the prairie.

"Mind if I ask you some questions?" Joe asked.

"About what?" Murray's tone was clipped and uninviting.

"Bernie Two Eagles."

Murray's gaze shifted from Gray back to Joe. "What about him?"

"Did you see him last night?"

"No, I was shut in my office all evening trying to catch up on my work. I've had to do too much on paper since Paul's death. Can't get into the accounting system no matter how hard I try." He turned to Gray. "When are we getting Paul's replacement? I'm desperate."

"I'm conducting interviews over the next week. I should have someone in two or three weeks tops."

Murray's mouth dropped open. "You don't understand. I needed someone two weeks ago, not two weeks from now." He shot a withering glare in Gray's direction. "It's not good enough. I can't do what you want me to do if I don't have the proper tools." Without sparing another glance at Joe, he spun on his heels and marched into his office.

"Kind of an intense guy, isn't he?" Joe mused.

"That's Murray. But he does the job." Gray's gaze probed the accountant's retreating figure. "Since he didn't see Bernie, I suppose you'll have to question the waitstaff.

I'm sure one of them will have seen him. If you'll excuse me, I need to have a word with our Mr. Murray." Gray disappeared into the office after Murray, his step firm as he closed the door behind him.

"Excuse me, Joe?" Gail Little Deer, dressed in a cocktail waitress's uniform, touched a hand to his arm.

"Hi, Gail, how's your mother?" Joe asked.

"She's doing much better without the kidney stones. She's home now and recuperating. Thanks for asking." She darted a look at the door Gray had gone into. "Could we…" She crooked her head to the side, "you know."

"Yeah." He walked with her farther down the hallway toward the rear exit. "What can I help you with?"

"Bernie was here last night really late. He was losing badly at the slots and kept going back to the teller machine to withdraw more money. I tried to get him to stop, but he wouldn't listen." Gail's forehead wrinkled into a frown and she stared up at Joe with sad, worried eyes. "I don't mind so much when I don't know the people, but Bernie was Lakota. One of us."

"Did he lose enough to want to commit suicide?" Joe asked.

"I don't know how much he lost. I finally asked Tom Little Elk to talk some sense into Bernie." She glanced down at her hands. "Tom was getting off work anyway so he promised to take him aside and walk him to his car. That was the last I saw of either one of them." She rested a hand on Joe's arm. "I heard about Tom. Do you think Bernie was mad at Tom for interfering and shot him, too?"

"We don't know what happened yet." But Joe didn't think Bernie could shoot anyone, especially not Tom.

The waitress wrung her hands, her eyes filling with tears. "It's my fault, isn't it? I should have butted out."

"Gail, you can't blame yourself for what happened." He reached out and patted her shoulder. "The best thing you can do is tell me everything you know."

She exhaled shakily. "I don't know much more than I've already told you."

"Do you know what time they left?"

"It was around twelve-thirty. Mr. Running Fox arrived with Mr. Caldwell right after Tom and Bernie left. I remember because I looked at the clock when they came in, thinking what a late dinner they'd had."

"Anything else?"

She glanced around the interior of the casino as if searching for any other shred of information. Finally, she sighed. "Not that I can think of."

"Well, if you do, you know where to find me."

She gave him a wan smile. "Hard to miss you in such a small community, Joe."

"Yeah, it is. Thanks, Gail." He reached out and squeezed one of her hands. "It's not your fault."

"Maybe not," she said. "But there have sure been a lot of people dying around here lately. I get the feeling not everything is as it appears."

Chapter Nine

"You gonna be all right, Mrs. Brandt?" Charlie asked, as he stood on the sidewalk outside the tribal police station waiting for his father.

Maggie closed the door behind her, her thoughts so many miles ahead she had to pull herself back into the here and now to answer him. "Yeah, Charlie. Only, I can't help thinking that if the Sukas are mad about the drugs, they might be the ones that took Dakota."

"Don't go messin' with the Sukas. They're a tough crowd. If they're the ones that kidnapped your kid, the tribal police and the FBI will find him. They're out there now, give them a chance." When Maggie didn't respond, Charlie gave her a hard stare. "You're not going to try to find the Sukas, are you?"

She reached out and squeezed the teen's shoulder. "Don't worry. I can take care of myself."

"Yeah sure, but you didn't answer me." He touched a hand to her arm. "Look, Mrs. Brandt—"

"Come on, Charlie." George Tatanka stepped out of the front door to the police station. "Let's get home. I gotta get to work in less than an hour."

Charlie hesitated, looking at Maggie with a frown.

"Oh, go on. I'm not going to do anything stupid." She crossed her fingers behind her back and waved with the other hand as father and son left in the back of the police vehicle in which they'd arrived.

As soon as they'd rounded the corner and disappeared, Maggie jumped in her little car and raced to the center for address information on Randy Biko. Assuming the Sukas had Dakota, as their leader, Randy would know where.

Rifling through her files, she pulled the one for Randy and spread it out across the desk. He'd been in the center to play basketball several times, but he hadn't committed to any kind of drug rehabilitation or counseling of any kind. Maggie sighed. She tried hard, but she couldn't get through to every kid.

In less than five seconds she'd transferred the address to a yellow sticky note and run back out to her car, her heart hammering in her chest. If Randy had her son, she could have him back within minutes.

That kind of belief was desperately optimistic. Nothing in the past few days had been easy thus far, why did she think it would change now? Still she couldn't help sending a silent litany of prayers to the heavens that Dakota was at Randy's home.

As she pulled onto a street with a mix of houses and mobile homes, she saw a dull gray rental car with an out-of-state license plate positioned a few doors down from the Bikos's vintage trailer. That had to be one of the FBI agents. Not a single car sat in the drive of the Biko home. If they had Dakota, they wouldn't have left him there. Maggie drove by, glancing briefly at the man behind the wheel of the sedan.

She recognized the agent who had interviewed her the day Dakota had disappeared, Chase Metcalf. Without pausing, she drove past and turned down the next street. A shiny black Mustang sat with a view through the dead weeds and trampled yards to the street where Biko lived.

Hadn't Maggie seen Kiya get into just such a vehicle on multiple occasions? Was it Randy's car? If so, he must have spotted the stakeout car on the next street and decided it wasn't safe to go home.

As the notion crystallized in Maggie's brain, the Mustang peeled out, leaving a layer of rubber on the rutted asphalt road.

Without a second thought, Maggie gunned her accelerator, holding tightly to the wheel as her little car leapt forward.

Taking the road leading into the hills, the Mustang sped up to over ninety miles an hour.

Never having gone more than eighty with the wind behind her, Maggie clung to the steering wheel, terrified she'd hit a patch of gravel and lose control of her compact car. But she couldn't let Randy get away. He was running from something and she would find out what it was, even if it killed her.

Before long, the road turned to gravel. She slowed to fifty miles per hour, falling farther behind the cloud of dust that was the black Mustang. Then the cloud and car ahead dipped below the horizon. What the heck?

Maggie pressed the accelerator and topped a rise so fast her car left the ground for a second, jolting back to earth and rattling every bone in her body. The road dropped downward into a canyon carved out of the earth by an ancient river.

She'd only been out this direction once over a year ago on a hiking trip with some of the younger kids from the center. One of the Lakota parents had acted as guide, leading them into and out of the twisting roads and trails. Now she was following a possible fugitive and couldn't remember her way around to save her life. But she'd come this far, and she wasn't going back without answers. Her foot pressed harder on the gas pedal and she urged her car faster. She had to catch up with the Mustang that had stirred the trail of dust now settling over the twisting and turning dirt road.

As she rounded a stand of rock formations, her foot jammed against the brakes and she skidded sideways.

Nine cars were parked to the side of the road. The black Mustang stood dead center in the middle of the gravel path, its front turned to face her little red compact car.

Teenagers she recognized and some she didn't stalked toward her car, closing in on the tiny compact.

Her heart rose into her throat and she fumbled for the shift, jamming it into Reverse.

When she looked into her rearview mirror, a beat-up elderly tank of a car had pulled in sideways behind her, blocking her way out.

Afraid more than she cared to admit, Maggie scrambled through her purse for her cell phone, trying to will herself to be calm, but failing miserably.

About twenty kids stood like a cloak around her vehicle. She couldn't get her car out with Randy parked in front of her and the tank behind her.

A quick glance down at her cell phone confirmed her fears. No little green bars lit up the screen. Even if she wanted to call for help, she couldn't. The walls of the canyon effectively blocked any reception she could hope to get on the South Dakota Indian Reservation.

What could she do? She tried to keep her expression calm as she cracked the window slightly and faced the boy she'd chased all the way here. "Randy, what's going on?" Despite her best efforts her voice shook.

"It's Snake," he corrected her. "And you tell me." His lip curled up in a sneer. "Why were you and that gook in the unmarked car hanging out by my place?"

What was the saying? A good defense was a good offence? Maggie shoved the door open and stood, immediately wishing she had stayed behind the relative safety of the metal doors of her car. However, if she wanted to find out where Dakota was, she had to get face-to-face with the person who might have him. "Where's my baby?"

Randy's eyebrows rose and he crossed his arms over his chest. "What's your kid got to do with me?" So he wanted to play dumb?

A glance around at the mix of guys and girls wearing droopy jeans and baggy jackets, most with piercings through various parts of their faces made Maggie's stomach churn. How could these kids who couldn't even take care of themselves responsibly take care of a small baby? She stood with her feet slightly apart, ready to do battle if she had to. "Please, if you have him, give him back."

Randy stared back at her. "We don't have your kid."

"I'm only here to find Dakota. If you know anything about his whereabouts, I need to know." Despite her determination to stay strong, tears welled in her eyes. "He's been missing since yesterday morning."

"Why should we help you?" Randy stepped closer. "You didn't help Kiya. Because of you, she's dead."

"What?" Maggie shook her head. "Why because of me? I tried to help her get off the drugs and get her life on track."

"Yeah? And where did that get her?" Randy pushed Maggie's shoulders so hard she slammed against her car.

"She died of an overdose." Maggie stared around the group of angry teens. "I didn't give her the drugs. How could you think I was responsible for her death? I tried to save her!" She stood straight and advanced on Randy as he'd done to her, her fear swallowed in self-righteous anger. "She'd gone through detox. Was that what made you mad? Did you give her the drugs that killed her? Because, if you did, you're responsible for her death, not me."

"I didn't give her that crap." Randy reached into the pocket of his jacket and pulled out a knife. "And I don't have to take this from you."

The knife and the twenty other teens surrounding her and her car didn't add up to very good odds for Maggie. She gulped and wished again she'd waited for Joe to return from the casino. "I'm not the cause of your problems, Randy, and only you can fix them."

"It's Snake, and yes you are. We were doing just fine before you came to the reservation. And I can't *fix* my problem. Kiya's dead. All I know is she wouldn't be dead if you hadn't butted in where you don't belong. We don't need no white woman telling us how to live. You don't know what it's like to spend your life on a reservation. You're not Lakota, so go home."

Randy's words hit her like a punch to the gut.

Another Lakota had once told her very much the same

words and broken her heart. She hadn't left then and she wasn't leaving now. "Not without my son."

As Joe climbed into his vehicle, his radio chirped on his shoulder. "Joe, this is Del."

"What is it, Del?" Joe answered immediately.

Delaney Toke was pretty laid-back for a cop, but he always showed proper protocol on the radio. Must be important if he'd cut through all the correct procedure and just call for Joe.

"Maggie's missing and I got a call from Charlie here at the station."

Joe's chest tightened. "What do you mean Maggie's missing?" he barked into the radio.

"That's what I'm trying to tell you. Charlie Tatanka called because he was afraid she might go after Randy Biko by herself."

"What?" Joe shoved his SUV into Reverse and jammed his foot on the accelerator, skidding out of the casino parking lot. "Where is she?"

"We aren't sure. Agent Metcalf was staking out Biko's place and thought he saw her pass through about thirty minutes ago."

"Did Randy ever show?"

"No," Del said. "Metcalf thinks Randy might have seen his car waiting there and taken off."

"And you think Maggie found him?" His heart slammed against his ribcage.

"I sent a unit by her house and she wasn't there. She's not at the center or the hospital with Winona and Tom."

"Damn," Joe muttered. "You don't think she went out to the Den, do you?"

"That was my first thought, so I sent a unit to check. They should be there about now."

As if on cue, the radio crackled. "This is unit four-five, Ms. Brandt is not at the Den. Any further instructions?"

Joe pressed the talk key, "Check the base of Black Butte, the Sukas used to hang out there." Frustration gnawed at Joe. Black Butte had been a Sukas hangout a year ago. Was it still? Being away so long from the reservation made him feel out of touch. He didn't know the gang haunts any more. "Del, where else?"

Joe headed back toward town, his speed creeping up to eighty, eighty-five. Where the hell was Maggie?

"I have people still going door-to-door looking for the baby, so I can't send another unit out looking for her. You might try Choke Canyon. I've heard the Sukas have been seen headed out that way lately."

"Roger. And if Maggie should come by the station while I'm out there, handcuff her to my desk, will you?"

Del emitted a very nonprocedural snort over the radio. "She'll love that. On what charges?"

"Being out of her mind, I don't know. Charge her with attempted murder. She's killing me here."

Del laughed into the radio, "Roger, Boss."

Joe raced west toward Choke Canyon. The sun had passed its zenith hours ago. With clouds moving in and days getting shorter, it would be dark within the next thirty or forty-five minutes. He hoped this was all a misunderstanding and that Maggie had only stopped at the grocery store for a can of soup or something. Surely she wasn't crazy enough to go after Randy "Snake" Biko alone? Guys like Biko were like dogs. They traveled in packs.

His stomach knotted. Packs had mob mentality written all over them. Kids did really stupid things when in groups, like taking drugs and knifing each other.

"Damn." Joe took the turn-off too fast and fishtailed on the gravel, struggling to retain control of the vehicle. If she was out at Choke Canyon, and if the gang was there…

His SUV flew along the gravel road, eating up the miles. Tall, brownish-yellow buffalo grass blurred in his peripheral vision.

He admitted he cared more than a tribal policeman would for a naive citizen. This was Maggie, the woman he fell in love with once. Who was he kidding? The truth was he'd never stopped loving her. He just didn't know what to do with that love.

He topped a short rise with enough speed to fly over the hump. Then the road led downward and he could see the canyon spread out before him. So far, no sign of vehicles. No sign of Maggie. There were a hundred places to hide in Choke Canyon. His ancestors had used the canyon walls to evade the government troops in the nineteenth century or to set up ambushes to trap them. Just as Randy and his followers could do. A lump of dread coursed through him.

When he reached the floor of the canyon, he slowed his vehicle to negotiate the narrow turns with more control.

Surely Maggie wouldn't have come this far. The farther he drove in, the easier he could breathe. No, this was a false trail, she wouldn't have come here.

About the time he came to that conclusion and was looking for a place to turn around, he rounded a corner and almost ran into a seventies-model rusted-out Buick LeSabre, turned sideways in the road.

Joe slammed on his brakes and slid to a halt two inches from contacting the peeling paint on the car's side panel.

A crowd of tough-looking teens stood in a circle around a bright-red compact car with a baby's car seat positioned in the middle of the back seat. Maggie stood outside next to the driver's door, her shoulders back, her face set in grim lines, a long, wicked blade pointed at her throat.

When Joe's SUV skidded to a stop behind the vehicle blocking Maggie's, teens dashed away.

Joe leaped from the SUV, pulling the Glock from the holster beneath his jacket. "Drop the knife, Randy," he said, striding toward the group and stopping short of the first teen.

"It's okay, Joe," Maggie called, her voice strained but in control. "Randy and I were just discussing things, weren't we?"

Randy shot a narrow-eyed look between Maggie's face and Joe's gun. For three or four long seconds he held the knife to her throat, and then his hand dropped to his side. "Yeah, sure." His thumb folded the blade back into the knife and he stuck it into his pocket. "She was just asking me if I'd seen her kid."

"And have you?" Joe asked, still holding the weapon pointed at Randy's chest in case he did something dumb. He didn't trust the crowd gathered around the lone woman. They were just kids, but their sullen faces and dark clothing were ominous in the confines of the canyon.

"No." The teen stared hard at Maggie.

"You don't need that, Joe," Maggie said, her face pale

beneath the freckles. "Randy and the rest of the Sukas were just leaving. Weren't you?"

"Yeah." Randy glanced around at faces too mean and fierce to be those of teens. "You heard it. We're leaving."

"Randy?" Maggie reached out and laid a hand on his arm.

The teen stared at her hand until she removed it. "The name's Snake."

Ignoring his comment, she continued, "Did you or any of your friends leave anything out at the Den?"

"I don't know nothin' about the Den. We don't hang there anymore." He jerked his head toward Joe. "Not since the police found it. As far as I know, no one does. Why?"

"No reason," Maggie said.

He shrugged and turned toward his Mustang. When he reached it, he pivoted and called out, "I hope you find your kid."

Once Randy settled behind the wheel of his vehicle, every engine revved and the sound reverberated off the sheer rock faces of the canyon walls. Following their leader, they filed out one by one until the only vehicles left were the little red compact and the tribal police SUV.

Joe stalked toward Maggie, his lips pressed together to keep him from shouting. When he stood in front of her, he let out a long-held deep breath. Then he launched into her. "What the hell did you think you were doing coming out here all alone?" He gripped her shoulders and shook her gently. "Those kids could just have easily stuck you with their knives and left you to bleed to death."

A tremor shook Maggie's body beneath his hands and she stared up at Joe. "I had to know. If there was even a slim chance of finding Dakota, I had to try." Her eyes filled with tears and she blinked them away.

"You should have left it to Agent Metcalf. He was tasked with interviewing Randy, not you."

"When I saw Randy's car, I don't know what came over me. I had to follow him out here. I thought maybe he would lead me to where Dakota was. But I was wrong." Her forehead dropped against his jacket. "They don't have Dakota and we're back to square one."

Her shoulders shuddered and then her entire body trembled with the force of her dry, wrenching sobs.

Joe pulled her against him and held her. Stroking a hand down her back, he muttered soothing words when all he wanted to do was shake her again. She could have been killed! And the thought made him shake in his own boots. An image of Maggie bleeding to death in this canyon almost brought him to his knees.

He couldn't lose her. She meant too much to him, and yet he had no claim to her, no right to be worried about her other than as the widow of his stepbrother and the mother of his nephew. She was just as unattainable to him as on the day he'd told her she didn't have a place in his life. And he found he wanted so much more of Maggie than he'd ever wanted to admit. The realization left him standing in a stupor, unable to move, lest he break the spell she'd cast on him.

When her crying stopped, her body continued to quiver.

Joe shook himself from thoughts of the woman he couldn't have and adjusted his focus to what was right for Maggie. "It's getting cold out here. Let's get you home." He walked her to her car when he wanted to tuck her into his and keep her within reach at all times. He had the uncontrollable fear that if he let her out of sight for a moment, something bad would happen.

He held her car door while she climbed in. "I'll lead the way out of here."

She laughed a short, humorless laugh. "Good, because I don't remember how I got in here. I was so intent on following Randy, I didn't stop to consider directions." She stared up at him with red-rimmed eyes. "I guess you think I'm pretty stupid."

"Yes." He leaned in the door and pressed a kiss to her lips. "Brave but stupid. Don't do it again."

Her lips curled into a soft smile that tugged at his heart. "Yes, officer," she said softly.

THROUGHOUT THE DRIVE back to Maggie's little house on Red Feather Lane, Joe pored over what Randy had said to her. He wondered if the young man had been lying or if he really didn't know where Dakota was.

When they arrived at Maggie's, Joe parked the SUV on the street, allowing Maggie to pull into the drive. As she inserted her key into the front door, Joe was there to enter before her to ensure there weren't any more surprises. He checked room by room, but the house was as they'd left it that morning. Another day had gone by and they still had no clue to the whereabouts of Dakota or what it was the kidnappers wanted in exchange for the baby, other than one really large bag of methamphetamines.

"Joe," Maggie trailed behind him into the master bedroom. "Do you think Randy was lying about the Den?"

His thoughts having just been through this process, he shook his head. "I don't know."

"I know." She sat on the edge of the bed they'd shared the night before, her back to him. "If the drugs weren't Randy's, who did they belong to?"

"I've been scratching my brain for the answer to that as well. And do the drugs have anything to do with Tom's injuries and Bernie's death?" Joe pulled the blinds away from the window and peeked out. "Based on what's been happening lately, I'm not so sure Paul's death was an accident." He turned back to her. "Did he mention anything about his work or extracurricular activities? Anything at all?"

"No." Maggie just shook her head. "We never talked."

He shook his head again. "You didn't have much of a marriage, did you, Maggie?"

She stared up at him, her mouth opening then closing before she finally said, "No, we didn't."

"I'm sorry." And he really was. Maggie had a big heart, as evidenced by her work with the kids at the center. And even after Randy'd held a knife to her throat, she'd been willing to let him go when she could have pressed charges.

She'd deserved better than an empty marriage. If they had been estranged for most of their time together, how had she and Paul come together long enough to have Dakota? Just the thought of Maggie in another man's arms made Joe's insides hurt. How could he be jealous of a dead man? He pushed the surge of unwanted emotion aside and tried to concentrate.

Perhaps her marriage had been better at first. Or maybe she'd married Paul on the rebound from him and it had all fallen apart when Dakota came along.

Poor kid. The child deserved a loving family like Joe'd had before his father died. Now the little boy was lost and his father was dead. Joe ached for the baby who was probably scared spitless and crying somewhere in the night—it was just like in Joe's dreams.

A tingle reached down his back and he shook it off. "You'd better get some rest. Tomorrow will likely be a long day for you."

"Do you really think they'll give me Dakota?" she asked, her voice barely a whisper.

When she looked up at him with green eyes bright with unshed tears, Joe did the only thing he could—he lied. "Yes." He had to get out of the room before he did anything else stupid.

"Joe?" Her call caught him before he cleared the doorway.

"Don't ask me to stay, Maggie," he said with his back to her. He couldn't stand lying next to her another night and not holding her close and loving her until her fears and tears went away. A man could take only so much before he lost control.

"Okay," she said, her voice swallowed by the chasm between them.

Then Joe did something he wished he hadn't. He turned to look back at her over his shoulder.

She sat on the edge of the bed, her hands clutched in her lap and her chin tipped downward. One giant tear after another rolled down her cheeks in silence.

He could have taken her anger or her indifference, but the silent tears were his undoing.

Get out, he told himself. *Get out, now.* He even took a step or two into the hallway before his feet made him do an about-face and he was back in the room, pulling Maggie into his arms.

Lifting her chin in his hands, he stared down at her watery green eyes. "I didn't want to do this." Then he kissed her, his lips crashing down on hers, his arms crushing her body to his.

Maggie's hands crept around his waist and held him tight, her fingers bunched in the back of his shirt.

His lips broke free and he forced himself to say, "I should go."

"No," she said, her voice a tiny puff of air against his lips. "Stay."

The way his instincts had overrun his common sense, he didn't need any more invitation. Maggie wanted him to stay and Joe wanted to stay more than he cared to admit. So what was holding him back?

He stopped kissing her and shoved her to arm's length. "What about Paul?"

Her mouth turned up in a wistful smile. "I loved Paul."

Joe dropped his hands from her arms, backing away as if he'd been sucker-punched in the gut.

"Wait, Joe." She still held him around the middle, keeping him from moving too far away. "I loved Paul like a brother, but I never fell in love with Paul."

"But he was the father of your son."

Maggie's arms stiffened around his waist and her face paled. Then she did let him go and turned away. "Joe, there's something you need to know."

"That you and Paul didn't have much of a marriage?" He wrapped his arms around her and pulled her back against his chest. "I can see that now. I'm sorry your life wasn't what it should have been. And I'm sorry if it was my fault. I made a mistake. I shouldn't have said what I did before I left."

Maggie spun in his arms and stared up into his face. "What do you mean?"

"I ran away from you, Maggie. You were everything I'd hoped to find in the woman I wanted to fall in love with."

"Except I wasn't Lakota."

He sighed. "I thought that was important. Ever since my father died, I wanted to hold on to everything that had to do with my ancestors, but the harder I tried, the more it slipped from my grasp. And then…"

"And then I came along and messed things up even further?"

"Yes." He pulled her close and kissed her on the lips. "But I was wrong. You care more about my people than most of the Lakota on the reservation. I just couldn't see that." He tipped her chin up so that she was looking straight into his eyes. "Will you ever forgive me?"

"I'll think about it," she said with a hint of a smile. Her eyelids drooped and her fingers worked the zipper of his jacket downward. Then those magical hands transferred to the buttons on his shirt.

Okay, so she hadn't said she'd forgive him. He'd have to earn her forgiveness by finding her son.

He didn't know how he'd *ever* walked away from this woman. All he knew for sure was that he couldn't walk away from her ever again. He grabbed the hem of her sweater and dragged it up over her head, exposing the frothy lace of her bra and pale skin lightly dusted with freckles.

Her fingers maneuvered his shirt from his shoulders,

and the belt from the loops around his hips, the long leather sliding through slowly with the promise of things to come.

Then she reached behind her and unclipped the back of her bra and her breasts spilled into his hands.

He reached out to cup her in his palms, twirling his thumbs across her nipples until they hardened into twin peaks.

Maggie wrapped her arms around his neck, pulling his head down to hers. With her lips hovering beneath his, she said, "Hold me, Joe." She tasted him with the tip of her tongue. "Hold me all night long."

The rest of their clothes hit the floor in a flurry of movement until they stood naked, clinging to each other.

Deep inside, a surge of desperation swelled in him, as if tonight was it. There would be no tomorrow for Joe and Maggie.

Chapter Ten

Maggie moaned when Joe bent to her breasts, laving first one then the other, pulling at the nipple and then sucking it in to fill his mouth.

She pressed closer, sliding her calf around the back of his leg until she rode his thigh, pressing him against her aching center.

Joe's hands curved around her hips and down over her buttocks and he lifted her. Wrapping her legs around his waist, he turned to lay her on the bed, climbing up to settle between her legs, his member poised at her entrance.

"Wait," she pushed against him. She might be crazy with lust for this man, but no way would she get pregnant again. Not with so much still up in the air. "What about protection?"

All the while Joe dug through his wallet and applied the condom he found, Maggie thought about why she shouldn't be doing what they were about to do, but she wanted to so badly. Having Joe inside her might help fill that cold empty space he'd left over a year ago and the emptiness of losing her child. She needed Joe tonight. Tomorrow would come and then she could tell him about his son.

And when Dakota was safe at home, they could finally be a family.

A tear leaked from the corner of her eye as Joe drove into her, filling her to full. He felt so good, so right inside her. But the cold reins of doubt held her back, refusing to let her love freely.

Her hands skimmed across his back and downward to clutch his buttocks, bringing him closer. Arching upward, she met him thrust for thrust, until they reached that peak and cried out, their bodies shuddering in the aftermath of their heated passion. Sweat mingled with tears and kisses with meaningless promises.

When Joe collapsed beside her on the bed, she kissed his lips and hooked a leg over him. "What time is it?" she asked sleepily.

"Past midnight. Why?"

"It's tomorrow," she said. "Dakota's coming home." Then she drifted to sleep held close in his arms.

JOE LAY skin-to-skin with Maggie, his hand resting on the swell of her hip. She was even more beautiful than the last time they'd made love over fourteen months ago. Before he'd left for Iraq. Before she'd married Paul and had a child with him. Fourteen months. She'd turned to Paul as soon as he'd gone and they must have made love immediately to produce a son so quickly.

Had he stayed, the child could have been his. Dakota could have been the son he'd always dreamed of. The one he'd raise as Lakota, learning the ways of his ancestors. He stared across the bed to the picture on the nightstand. Maggie held Dakota, the love evident in the way she smiled down at her son. His hair, like a cap of peach fuzz, shone with a red tint like his mother's and his eyes were dark-brown. Would he resemble Paul, with his blond hair and blue eyes, or Maggie with her deep auburn hair and green eyes? Just by looking at the picture, Joe couldn't tell. If Dakota had half the heart of his mother, he'd grow into a good man. A man a father would be proud of. Would his father have been proud of the way he'd treated Maggie? Joe knew in his heart that his father would have been disappointed.

Lying in his tent in Iraq, Joe had dreamed of holding Maggie, and now that he was, he couldn't imagine ever letting her go again. But he wasn't sure she was ready to let him back into her life on a more permanent basis. Although she'd given herself freely tonight, she still held back and rightfully so. She had a child to think about and he'd let her down before. What had he done to prove he wouldn't do it again?

He stared at the clock on the nightstand. One o'clock on day three and he still hadn't found Maggie's son. Who would have taken a small child?

Randy Biko said he didn't have him and he was the closest person to a suspect they had. Then there were the happenings at the casino. Was Bernie's "suicide" a cover-up for something else? Did Bernie have a fallout with Tom and shoot him in a rage?

No. Bernie wasn't the violent type. If not Bernie, then who? Could someone at the casino have killed Bernie and tried to kill Tom as well? And did Paul's death have any connection? The more he sifted through the pieces of in-formation, the more certain he became that something was not as it seemed at the casino.

The digital alarm on the bedside flipped over to two

o'clock. Joe yawned and closed his eyes. He'd go back to the Grand Buffalo and poke around some more in the morning. There had to be something there. His last thought as he drifted into sleep centered on the woman he held in his arms and how she must have looked swollen with child. Probably sexy as hell. He wished he had been there to see her like that. And more than anything, he wished Dakota had been his.

JOE CROSSED the moonlit prairie, riding bareback astride a painted pony. His black hair was longer than he'd worn it since he was a boy, before his father died. The strands brushed over his shoulders, flowing in the breeze. In the distance was a lone house rising out of the tall grasses. As he approached, he reined in the horse, bringing him to a halt. Charlie Tatanka stood before him, a smile of welcome on his face as he waved his hand toward the house.

Joe slid from his pony and walked barefoot through the fresh green grass of spring. Before he reached the door, a woman stepped out.

Maggie. She wore the bright colored dress of Lakota Indian women, her wild red hair tamed into twin braids caressing her cheeks. As she reached out her arms, a small child slipped around her legs and ran toward him whooping like an Indian brave, "Papa! Papa!"

His heart filled with pride and the warmth of coming home to a family he loved. When he leaned down to lift the little boy into his arms, the vision disappeared, the boy vanished and Maggie called out into the void, "Joe!"

Everything was black, like the darkest starless night,

and silent except for the electronic music of slot machines. Although he couldn't see where he was, he knew he was in the casino and something horrible lurked in the darkness, just beyond reach. He fumbled along the walls looking for the light switch until he bumped into a soft mound on the floor. Dropping to his knees, his hands traced along arms and legs to the person's neck and he felt for a pulse. Nothing, and his skin was as cold as the prairie earth in winter.

Who was this man and why was he here at the casino? Joe stood and felt again along the wall until he finally found a light switch. Flipping it up, he stared at the ground. Where the body had been was nothing except a red stain on the multi-colored carpet.

A child cried and Joe turned toward the gaming room, the lights blinding him. The child's screams became more terrified and Joe ran into the maze of slot and video poker machines. The more the child cried, the deeper he went into the neverending rows of gambling devices. The ringing grew louder and louder until his eardrums neared bursting.

He squeezed his eyes shut and slapped his palms to his ears. When he thought he'd go crazy with the cacophony of sounds, a sweet voice called out to him.

"Joe."

His eyes opened to clean white walls kissed by morning light.

Maggie was sitting up in bed shaking his shoulder, clutching a sheet to her naked breasts.

A dream. It was just a dream. As he unclenched his fists, the ringing started again. Or was this the dream, lying in bed with a naked Maggie beside him?

"Joe," she said, a frown deepening the lines over her forehead. "Your cell phone's ringing."

Immediately alert, he sat up and grabbed for the phone, flipping it open. "Yeah."

"We have a lead on who might have made that meth."

"I'll be right in." He disconnected the call and grabbed for his clothes. "I have to go."

MAGGIE HUGGED the sheet to her chest, amazed she could be shy after what they'd done the night before. "Any news on Dakota?" she asked, knowing he'd have said something if the call had had anything to do with her son.

This was the third morning she'd gotten up without her son.

Joe came to her, zipping his uniform trousers. He bent to press a kiss to her lips. "No, Maggie. No word on Dakota, yet. I got a lead on who might have made the methamphetamines. I'm going to follow up on it and see if this person might be our kidnapper."

"I'm going with you," she shoved the sheets aside, all modesty gone with the possibility of finding Dakota.

Joe rested his hands on her waist, his gaze running the length of her body.

Maggie quivered with the need she thought she'd satisfied the night before. How could she want him so soon after making love? *Because he's always been a part of you. Because you love him.* Her breath caught in her throat at the strength of her conviction. She'd always loved Joe, even more than life itself. If Dakota hadn't come along, she didn't know how she could have gone on without Joe.

"Much as I want you with me, it might not be safe. I'll drop you at the station as soon as you're dressed and you can wait there until I get back. I don't feel comfortable with you being alone." He kissed her full on the lips, his hands rising up her back, pulling her closer until he crushed her naked breasts against his shirtless chest. "Promise me one thing," he said, his lips brushing against hers.

Standing like this with him, she was likely to promise him anything he wanted.

"Promise me that we'll talk later."

Oh, yeah. The talk. The big reveal about the true lineage of her son and what they were going to do about it. "I promise." She had to tell him, but not while they were running out the door. Timing never seemed to be right for this big a revelation.

He held her tight against him, the hard ridge behind his zipper pressing into her belly. He still wanted her.

A thrill of anticipation raced across her skin. Maybe the next time they made love, Dakota would be home in his bed and Joe would have forgiven her for not telling him about his son.

And pigs might learn to fly.

In less than two minutes, Maggie was dressed, clad in snow boots and zipping her jacket as she exited her house. "I'll follow you in my car," she called out.

Joe frowned. "I'm not sure I trust you to have your own car."

"Don't go native on me. I don't like being stranded at the station all day. Besides, I need to run by the center for a few minutes."

"I kinda like the idea that you'll be stranded. It keeps

me from worrying you'll follow up some wild hare-brained scheme you get."

"Don't worry. I learned my lesson about following snakes into canyons." A smile quirked the corners of her lips and then faded. "Go on, I want my son back today."

Joe hesitated a moment longer, and then climbed into his SUV. He waited on the street for Maggie to back out and followed her all the way to the center, where they split up and Joe went on to the station.

Maggie breathed a sigh of relief. She had some things she wanted to check on and Joe would most likely stop her if he knew.

WHEN JOE ENTERED the station, Chase Metcalf stood from the desk where he'd plugged in his laptop. He held out a sheet of paper. "Check this out."

Joe took the sheet and looked it over.

"I ran a scan on people with felony convictions in the area. I'm running a scan on some of the casino employees you mentioned, expanding the search to nationwide."

Joe recognized some of the names for shoplifting, hot checks and possession, but one name stuck out. "Bill Franks. Hey, Del, ever heard of Bill Franks?"

"Isn't he the guy that delivers the snacks for the vending machines around here and out at the Grand Buffalo?"

"That's what I thought. Says here he was convicted of possession five years ago." Joe's brow lifted. "Any idea of what?"

"Let me check. The state police picked him up on that charge." Del dropped into his desk chair and pounded a few keys on the terminal. After several long minutes, he looked up, his face set grimly. "Seems our man Franks was convicted of possession of cocaine. Spent time in the state prison. He was released eight months ago."

"How does a guy who's been convicted of drug possession get a job running vending machines all over the reservation? He could be delivering drugs to every teen around."

Del shrugged. "Maybe he's part of a rehabilitation program?"

"For the person or for reestablishing the drug trading?" Joe muttered. "I saw him out at the casino yesterday when I was there to speak with the manager, Gray Running Fox."

"Think he has something to do with that bag of ice that Charlie Tatanka found?" Metcalf asked.

"I don't know, but it wouldn't hurt to ask," Joe said. "Del, call the vending machine company and find out what his route is?"

"Sure thing." Del swiveled in his chair and keyed up the online phone book.

"Anything on Maggie's kid?" Joe sat at his desk and rifled through the reports from his deputies who'd been knocking on doors for two days now.

"Nothing," Metcalf answered. "We've exhausted all the occupied houses on the reservation. The state police are checking the homes in the area immediately adjacent to the reservation. If the kid's in one of them, we'll find him. Isn't she supposed to make the exchange tonight?"

"Yeah. But I'm still not sure the drugs are what they're after. The timing isn't right." Joe tapped a pencil to the stack of files littering his desk. "The baby was stolen before Charlie took the bag. It doesn't add up."

Metcalf leaned back in his chair. "Unless someone like Paul Brandt took the drugs first."

"I'd thought of that," Joe said. "But why wait so long to come after them?"

Metcalf drummed his fingers against the desktop for several seconds before responding. "Maybe the dealer didn't realize the drugs were missing until recently?"

"There's a lot of money involved in such a big stash. Surely the dealer kept closer tabs on it than that." Joe stood. "I'd like to get hold of Bill Franks and see what he knows."

Del hung up the phone he'd been speaking into and announced, "Franks should be making a delivery at the casino in the next hour."

"Good, I have a couple more questions to ask Gray and his colleagues."

"Want me to come?" Del rose from his chair and grabbed his jacket.

"No, I'm going to swing by the hospital to see if Tom Little Elk is awake yet, then I'll head to the casino. Maggie's supposed to come over right after she gets done at the center. Your job is to keep an eye on her."

"Thanks." Del grinned. "I love to play babysitter to good-looking women."

Joe glared at Del.

The police officer raised his hands. "Okay, okay. I get the message. Watch but don't touch. Didn't know she was your territory."

Joe's tension released and he sighed. "She's not."

"Yeah, right." Del laughed. "Should I go over to the center and keep an eye on her there to be on the safe side?"

"That's not a bad idea." Joe would have gone by there himself, but he needed time away from her to think.

MAGGIE THUMBED through the files in her four-drawer file cabinet on the kids that had been in and out of trouble for the past ten years since the center had been open. The prior social worker had retired to Rapid City to take care of her aging mother, leaving the records in good shape. Maggie had no problem going through them.

"Mrs. Brandt?"

The file she'd been holding slipped from her fingers and Maggie stifled a scream. Spinning around, she gave a nervous laugh when she saw it was only Charlie standing in the doorway to the office. "Charlie, don't do that!" She inhaled and let out a lungful of air before she schooled her face into calm.

"I didn't mean to scare you." The teen squatted to retrieve the papers. "I should have knocked."

"Or stomped your feet coming across the basketball court or cleared your throat…anything. I think you knocked ten years off my life." Why was she so jumpy? Probably because two people had died in the past two weeks and her child was missing?

Charlie straightened and handed her the file. "If now's not a good time, I'll come back."

"No, no. Please come in." She stuffed the papers back in the folder and replaced them in the file cabinet before she turned to Charlie with a smile. "I'd hoped I'd see you today."

"Really?" Charlie lifted a snow globe of Mount Rushmore from her desk and tipped it over. "I heard you went out to Choke Canyon yesterday to find Snake."

"Who told you?" Maggie asked.

The fake snowflakes swam down over the faces of the presidents before he looked up. "Snake."

"Oh my God, are you all right?" She walked around her desk and reached for Charlie, holding him at arm's length, checking for any signs of harm.

The teen shook her hands from his shoulders and set the snow globe back on her desk. "I'm okay."

"Randy didn't hurt you?"

"No. But I don't need you looking out for me. I can take care of myself." His face looked stubborn for a moment and then it cleared. "I also found out Snake didn't give Kiya the drugs."

"That's what he told me," Maggie said. "Did you believe him?" Randy had seemed so sincere about Kiya yesterday, Maggie had swallowed his line. She tensed waiting for Charlie's response.

The boy nodded. "I believe him. I was so mad about Kiya's death, I wanted to blame someone, and the only one I could find to blame was Snake. I guess not everything is what it looks like."

"Then who gave her the drugs that killed her?"

"Snake thinks it was the pusher that used to supply them." Charlie dug his hands into his jacket. "I'm probably telling you too much."

"No!" Maggie almost reached out to Charlie again, but thought better and gripped her hands together behind her back. "This could make the difference in finding my son. Please tell me what you know. What pusher, Charlie?"

He shot a glance over his shoulder as if someone might

be listening in to his confession and he edged farther into the room. "Someone they call Tokala."

Maggie shook her head, the Lakota words she'd learned since she'd moved to the reservation rattling around, but none sounded like *Tokala*. "What does that mean?"

Charlie shrugged. "I don't know. I guess it's a Lakota word for something."

"Did they say where you could find Tokala?"

"Snake said Tokala spends time out at the casino. That's all he knew. Tokala usually finds them, not the other way around."

The casino.

"I gotta go. I just wanted you to know the Sukas aren't gonna bother me. But I'm not sure who is. I almost think not knowing who's after you is worse."

"Have you told the tribal police? Did you tell Joe?"

"Not yet. I thought I'd let you know and you could tell them. I have to get to work." He eased toward the exit. "I've missed too much time already. My boss won't like it if I miss more."

Maggie walked with Charlie to the door leading to the parking lot, hope bubbling inside her.

Before he opened the door, Charlie turned back to her. "You'll tell Officer Lonewolf what I said?"

"Yes, Charlie. I'll tell him."

Once Charlie left, Maggie raced back to her office, grabbed her purse and jacket and ran out of the building headed for her car. If Charlie was right and the man who wanted the meth was out at the casino, she might not have to wait until midnight to get Dakota back.

Chapter Eleven

Winona Little Elk met Joe in the hall when he arrived at the hospital. "I just had lunch in the cafeteria. Did they tell you Tom woke up for a few minutes?" Her face was wreathed in smiles as she hurried along beside Joe.

"No, I hadn't heard." Joe slowed his steps to match Winona's short legs. Maybe Tom could tell them more about the attack. "That's good news. I'm happy for you."

"He didn't stay awake long. The doctors have him sedated for the pain."

"Where was he hit?" Joe asked.

"Once in the shoulder and a bullet grazed his temple. He's lucky he's so darned hardheaded." Winona's footsteps faltered. "Or he might not have made it." Tom and Winona had been sweethearts since their school days some forty years ago. Losing Tom would have been a huge blow to Winona. They'd been inseparable for most of their lives.

Had Joe's father lived, Joe was certain his parents would have had the same lasting relationship. And that was the kind of relationship Joe had always wanted. And he could have had it with Maggie if he hadn't missed his chance. "Did Tom say anything about who shot him?"

"No. He didn't see who did it. He'd just stepped out of his car at the house when he was attacked." She gripped Joe's arm with her dark pudgy fingers, stopping him in the hallway. "I heard the gunshots and thought it was someone's car backfiring. I didn't think anything of it for the first fifteen minutes." Her eyes filled. "My poor Tom was lying out in the cold for fifteen minutes and I was watching the television."

"You couldn't have known. And what matters is that he's going to be okay."

She ignored his words, her chin dropping to her ample chest. "It wasn't until he was fifteen minutes past time to get home before I looked outside and saw his car sitting there in the drive with the door wide open." She stared up at him. "What's happening around here, Joe? First Paul, then little Dakota and now Bernie and Tom. I'm afraid to step outside anymore. It shouldn't be that way."

Joe pulled the short, round woman into his arms and held her close for several minutes. He'd known Winona all his life—she'd been there for him when his father died and when his mother had passed away three years ago. "I don't know what's happening yet, but it's going to stop if I have anything to do with it."

Winona stepped out of Joe's arms and, pulling a clean tissue from the pocket of her trousers, she dabbed at the moisture on her cheeks. Then she continued down the hallway.

Joe followed.

"I hope you fix it soon, Joe. We can't rest until whoever

did this is found and that sweet baby is back in his mother's arms." She stopped outside the door to a patient's room and stared up at Joe. "Speaking of Dakota, did Maggie ever tell you why she married Paul?"

Joe's lips twisted. "Yeah, she did." She'd done what he'd expected and married someone who wasn't Lakota. Hell, he'd driven her into an unhappy marriage to the brother he'd never wanted to claim until it was too late.

"All the more reason to find that baby, then, huh?" Winona patted his arm. "I told her you'd understand. Let me check and see if my Tom's awake." The older Lakota woman ducked into the room and was back in less time than it took for Joe to pull his head out of his thoughts of Maggie.

"Tom's still asleep. Want me to call when he comes around?"

"Please." He'd sure like to know what the connection was to Tom and Bernie other than the supposed chat about gambling.

Maybe Gray Running Fox and Mr. Caldwell could add to the picture. If they came in about the time Bernie and Tom left the casino, they might have seen something suspicious. He should have asked on his last visit to the casino. However, this way, he had an excuse to be hanging around the casino when Bill Franks made his delivery.

MAGGIE SLIPPED in through a smaller side entrance, feeling silly about being so cloak-and-dagger. The casino was a public place and she wasn't afraid of being there. Her greatest terror was that she'd frighten off the person who had her baby if he saw her first. Surely he wouldn't hide a baby in the casino, would he?

With her red hair tucked neatly under a wool cap, she hoped she wouldn't stand out in the casino scattered with white-haired retired folks.

Most people her age were working their day jobs and couldn't afford the time during the week to gamble at the casino. The way Maggie saw it, as long as her baby was missing, her day job could take a hike.

Her footsteps dragged.

Who was she trying to kid? If the teens needed her, she'd be as open to them as she'd always been.

After Joe's rejection, when she would rather have run away with her tail between her legs, she'd stayed at the reservation. Kiya, Charlie and a dozen other teens needed her. She couldn't run out on them. It was her job to help them through their problems.

But who had helped her through hers?

Paul had tried to help her get over her broken heart. But Joe wasn't the kind of guy she could forget in a hurry. After fourteen months, she should have been well over him. Unfortunately, she wasn't even close to erasing him from her mind or heart. She wanted him now more than ever.

As she worked her way through the rooms full of nickel slot machines, Maggie peered closely at the casino employees. Most were the dark-skinned, brown-eyed Lakota Indians from the Painted Rock Reservation. She hoped she could find one she knew from her work at the center.

Walking through the bays of dollar slots and video poker, she paused every now and then to slide a dollar into a machine and pretend she was playing while she thought through her plan.

What plan? How in the hell was she going to find a drug

dealer named Tokala when he probably didn't go by that name other than when he dealt drugs? As the reservation social worker, whose job it was to reform drug-abusing teens, Maggie bet Tokala wouldn't be interested in talking to her. Especially since she was trying her darnedest to put him out of business. He'd want his stash, not words.

She chewed on her lip and pressed the spin button, looking around at the people wandering from one machine to another. Waitstaff moved among the customers, providing drinks and change for the gamblers and occasionally directions to the nearest restroom.

"Need change?" A young woman in a short black skirt and uniform top pushed her change cart up next to the machine where Maggie lingered. "Oh, hello, Mrs. Brandt."

Okay, so her disguise wasn't all that great if the first person she talked to knew her. Maggie pulled her searching gaze from the open bay to the girl standing in front of her.

Rebekah Black Bear was one of the young women who used to hang out at the center until she'd turned twenty-one last year and landed a job at the Grand Buffalo Casino.

"Hi, Rebekah."

"Is this your first time here?" she asked, her smile genuine and welcoming. "Maybe there's something I could help you with."

"As a matter of fact, there is." Maggie wondered how much she could say and not scare the girl off. "You used to hang out with the Sukas, didn't you?"

Rebekah's smile faded and she glanced around her as if afraid of being overheard. "I'd rather keep that between you and me." She nodded at a stooped old woman ambling by with her plastic casino bucket full of quarter tokens for the slots. "Hi, Mrs. Humbolt. Having a good time?"

"Danged machines are tight today," Mrs. Humbolt muttered as she shuffled by to another row of machines across the aisle.

Rebekah leaned close. "Management doesn't like their employees associated with gangs. Not good for business. Besides, I quit them over a year ago."

"I know, and I'm sorry to bother you." Maggie had seen this girl turn completely around from a gang-running teen, experimenting in every kind of drug from marijuana to meth, to a working mother trying to earn a degree through an online university. Raising a baby on your own had a way of forcing you to grow up. "I wouldn't bother you if it wasn't important. I'm looking for a man called Tokala. Have you heard of him?"

The girl's dusky complexion paled. "No. No I haven't." She kicked the brake off the cart and leaned into it. "I have to go now."

"Please, Rebekah. If you can tell me anything about him, I need to know. I think he took my baby."

Rebekah stopped and turned toward Maggie, a sad frown pushing her black eyebrows together. "I'm sorry about your baby, but I can't help you. And if I were you, I wouldn't ask around. It might be dangerous." Before Maggie could respond, Rebekah wheeled away her change cart, its rotating amber light blinking brightly in the semi-dark room.

Tokala must mean bad medicine if it could scare Rebekah Black Bear away. And if she was right, asking around might only land Maggie in more trouble. Maggie felt in her bones that there was more to the casino than bright lights and noise. Her son's kidnapper had to be here or connected to the place in some way, and she wasn't leaving until she learned more.

She made her way through the doors marked Employees Only and back through the kitchens and laundry facilities for the hotel. Along the way, she ducked her head when she passed people in the hallway, but no one stopped to ask who she was or why she was wandering around in the bowels of the casino. Once or twice she almost got up the nerve to ask someone else if they knew of a man called Tokala, but Rebekah's words stilled her tongue and she moved on, peering into every face she passed, hoping someone would jump out as Tokala.

Frustration welled up in her about the time she came to the back loading docks. A man in khaki trousers and matching jacket stood next to a hand truck loaded with a stack of boxes. His hair needed a cut and he had that hard-faced look of someone she wouldn't want to meet in a back alley. He pointed his finger at each box and counted aloud, then stared at the sheet in front of him. "One more of the Sunshine Chips."

With no idea where she was and no one else to ask, Maggie chewed her bottom lip and reviewed her options. She could go home with no more information on the whereabouts of her son or she could ask this man if he knew anything about Tokala. Or the better choice was to go back into the guest side of the hotel and ask some of the other workers if they knew about Tokala.

She opened her mouth to ask the man in front of her the question burning a hole in her tongue.

But the man in the khaki uniform shot what had to be

classified as a contemptuous glance her way and exited through a door that led down a ramp outside.

Well! He didn't have to practically glare at her. So she didn't belong in this part of the casino, big deal. Her son was missing and she wanted answers. Maggie squared her shoulders and awaited the man's return.

When he appeared in the doorway with his arm curled around a box, he spotted her still standing there and scowled. "What do you want?"

"Have you heard of a man called Tokala?" she blurted out before she lost her nerve.

His eyes flared, before they narrowed into tiny slits. He looked as though he could melt nails with one look. "Aren't you that socialist who works with the kids at the center?"

"Yes, I mean no. I'm not a socialist, I'm a social worker. I'm Maggie Brandt. I'm looking for a guy called Tokala. Do you know of him?"

He crossed his arms over his chest. "Maybe I do, and maybe I don't."

Maggie wanted to stomp her foot on the man's smug expression. "Look, buddy. Tokala might be the guy who took my son, and I want my boy back."

He pulled a toothpick out of his pocket and stuck it between his lips. "Sounds like you have a problem," he said around the toothpick.

"Do you or don't you know a man named Tokala?"

"Maybe."

Steam could have risen from the top of Maggie's head as she clenched her hands into fists to keep from grabbing the man and shaking him.

"Well, if you know him, tell him this: I have what he's

looking for and if he wants it, he'd better be at the base of Coyote Butte tonight. With my son. If he isn't, I'll give it to the police. Got it?"

The man laughed, the sound grating like the voice of someone who'd smoked a few too many cigarettes. "Yeah. I got it."

Her son wasn't there, the man wasn't talking, and discretion played the better part of valor. Maggie turned and retreated in the direction from which she'd come.

JOE CIRCLED the entire casino compound looking for the Vend-a-Snack truck. At the rear entrance loading ramps he spotted it backed against a loading dock, a man walking down the ramp of the truck carrying a box.

It had to be Franks.

Parking his tribal police SUV around the corner from the dock, Joe entered the casino and made his way to the back of the building where he knew he'd find Bill Franks and his boxes of snacks. Just what kinds of snacks were in the boxes was yet to be determined.

As he headed through the building to the back loading ramp, he could hear voices ahead; one of them sounded like Maggie's.

His strides lengthened as her voice rose. He couldn't quite make out her words, but he could tell she was angry. Her anger didn't hold a candle to Joe's.

What the hell did she think she was doing coming out to the casino by herself? He stopped short of the corner around which he guessed was the loading dock. Footsteps pounded toward him. Someone who didn't weigh much and took shorter strides than a man.

He ducked out of sight just as Maggie strode by, her mouth firm and her green eyes flashing fire. She was gorgeous when she was mad. When she disappeared through the swinging doors leading toward the office area, Joe turned back the way she came and almost ran into a man pushing a cart filled with boxes of snack foods.

Joe peered around the boxes at the man behind the cart. His face was lined and leathery like a person who'd smoked all his life. Dark hair was slicked back from his forehead. He wore an earring in his left ear and had a tattoo on his neck. This was the man Maggie was yelling at? Joe almost grinned. The girl had a lot of spunk and possibly a death wish. "Bill Franks?" Joe asked.

"Who wants to know?"

"Officer Lonewolf, tribal police." Joe held up his badge. "Would you answer a few questions for me?"

Bill snorted. "You got a warrant? Am I under arrest?"

Joe sighed impatiently. "No, I don't have a warrant and no, you're not under arrest."

"Then talk to my lawyer or arrest me. I ain't answering anything. Now, if you'll move, I got work to do."

Franks walked away, pushing his cart through the corridor.

Joe had a good mind to arrest the bastard and haul his butt down to the station for questioning. But first, he had to find Maggie and make sure she wasn't getting herself into more of a mess. And when he found her, he'd get to the bottom of why she was arguing with Franks.

MAGGIE WAS HOT after her conversation with the chips man, and she wasn't really keeping track of where she was going until she noticed a sign reading Casino Manager, with an arrow pointing down a corridor to her left. Maybe someone in the casino management could tell her where to find Tokala. Still full of steam, Maggie marched down the passageway. The farther she went the more her anger evaporated, and she glanced back every time she thought she heard a sound.

"I don't have time for this, Leotie." A deep male voice said from the doorway ahead.

"You're not going to ignore me anymore. We're a team, remember? You need me."

"The only team here is in your head." The man's voice was incensed, almost snarling. "And don't threaten me."

Knowing she was somewhere she shouldn't be, overhearing a private conversation, Maggie looked for a place to hide to avoid detection. She ducked behind a huge potted tree and crouched low to the floor.

Leotie Jones, wearing a short black skirt and a go-to-hell-red suit jacket buttoned tightly over a low-cut cream camisole, stepped out of the door followed by Gray Running Fox. The man's face was creased in a fierce frown.

"I don't plan on spending my next thirty years on this dump of a reservation. If I don't get my money, I'll—"

Gray reached out and slapped Leotie's face. "Shut up. Just shut up."

Maggie gasped and clapped a hand to her mouth. When she crouched even lower, her purse slipped from her shoulder and dropped to the marble tile with a soft thump.

Gray shot a look in her direction.

She sank lower behind the giant planter and held her breath. Could he see her in the little alcove behind the tree? What would she say if she got caught? "Excuse me. I was looking for the restroom and fell behind the tree."

"Get in my office." He stepped aside to make room for Leotie to pass by, all the while scanning the hallway.

"No." The young Native American woman didn't budge. "You can't order me around anymore. I won't let you."

Gray's face reddened as he stared down at the stubborn woman. Then he grabbed her hand and jerked her into his office, slamming the door closed.

Unsure how long they'd be in the office, Maggie searched the corridor for a better hiding place. A room on the opposite wall from her was marked Janitorial Supplies. After a quick glance at the door where Gray and Leotie had gone, she dashed across the hall and into the janitor's supply closet. Before she could turn to close the door, someone plowed into her from behind and clamped a hand over her mouth, stifling her automatic scream.

The door closed and the room was plunged into complete and utter darkness.

With her heart beating wildly against her ribcage and a man's breath blowing hot against her neck, Maggie struggled to free herself or at least to free her mouth to scream bloody murder. Remembering the training she'd received in the self-defense class she'd taken in college, she jabbed her elbow into his solar plexus.

And it worked! The man doubled over, muffling a grunt into the back of her shoulder, his hot, moist breath gusting warm against her collar.

Then she jammed her heel into the man's instep. His hand loosened around her mouth and she twisted around in the dark intent on finishing the job with a palm heel to the nose and a quick knee to the groin.

Before she could jam her palm into his face, he gasped, "Maggie, it's me, Joe."

"Joe?" Her hand halted in mid-thrust. "Why the hell did you push me into a closet?" she said, loud enough to get her point across, but not loud enough to be heard on the other side of the door.

"I was about to let you know I was behind you when I heard someone coming out the door of Gray's office. I thought it better to shove now and explain later."

Maggie really didn't care. Now that she knew it was him, she was glad he was there. Her encounter with the chip man and her near miss with Gray and Leotie had shaken her more than she'd initially thought. She leaned against Joe for a few moments, soaking in the scent of his leather jacket and the crisp smell of the outdoors. "Did you see the way he treated her?"

"The way who treated whom?" he asked, his hands rising around her back, pulling her even closer.

"Leotie. Gray slapped her full in the face." As Maggie's eyes adjusted to the limited lighting creeping up from the gap beneath the door, she could see Joe's outline and just his presence made her feel less afraid. "We should go out there and tell him to leave her alone."

Angry voices sounded in the hallway and Maggie strained to hear the words.

"I'm not one of your employees who will do anything you want, so don't threaten me." Leotie's voice was loud and emotional.

Gray's was more controlled and harder to make out

through the thick metal of the door. Maggie pressed her ear to the cool door.

"What are you doing?" Joe asked.

"Shhh. I'm listening."

"That's eavesdropping." He pressed his ear to the door, their noses practically touching.

"I want to make sure he isn't hurting her." She wanted to rush out and punch the guy in the gut. But not as much as she wanted to lean forward and kiss Joe just for being there. "No matter how ugly Leotie's been to me, she doesn't deserve to be slapped around by a man twice her size."

"She's been ugly to you?" Joe asked.

"Shhh." Her and her big mouth. Now he'd demand an explanation of how Leotie had been ugly to her. Maggie sure as hell didn't plan on telling him anything about that particular conversation.

The voices moved away and the corridor was silent beyond the door.

"Think she'll be okay?" Maggie turned to Joe and found him a lot closer than she'd anticipated. So close that when he leaned slightly forward, his chest touched hers.

"How do you do that?" He tipped her face up to his. His eyes looked black in the near-dark of the closet.

With the warmth of his hand on her face, she could barely breathe. "How do I do what?" she managed to respond despite the confusion his nearness inspired in her thoughts.

"How do you care so much about people even when they aren't very nice to you?"

She stared up into the shadow of his face, mesmerized by the sound of his voice. "Everyone has a reason for acting the way they do. I only give them the benefit of the doubt."

"Will you give me the benefit of a doubt, as well?" He cupped her face in his palm before his lips descended to capture hers.

For a few long moments, Maggie was lost in a world beyond the janitor's closet. One where she held her heart's desire in her arms and kissed him until her head spun. When they broke apart, Joe kissed her forehead and brushed her lips with his. "I've missed you, Maggie. Can you forgive me for being such a jerk before I left? Please say you will."

"I missed you, too." Then Maggie crashed back to earth and remembered why she couldn't be free to love Joe. She hadn't told him the secret she'd kept from him for all these months.

"Joe, I…" The words caught in her throat. How could she give him the forgiveness he wanted when she hadn't told him about Dakota? And she couldn't bring herself to tell him yet. The timing wasn't right. Not in a janitor's closet hiding from the management of a casino. He deserved better.

"Never mind, we can work things out later." His grip on her arms tightened. "Now tell me why you were arguing with Bill Franks at the loading dock."

Chapter Twelve

"Is that who that was?"

"Yeah, and he has a rap sheet a mile long." He rubbed his hands down her arms. "He's spent time in prison recently. I'd say he's probably dangerous."

Maggie drew in a deep breath and slowly let it out. "I was trying to find Dakota and the jerk wouldn't answer my questions."

Despite his concern over her discussion with ex-con Bill Franks, Joe couldn't help a soft chuckle. Maggie could be a hellcat when she was fighting for someone she loved. "You really need to know who you're talking to before you pick a fight."

"Why, who's Bill Franks, anyway? The name doesn't ring a bell."

"You probably don't recognize his name because Bill Franks had been in prison when you came to Painted Rock. He's a recent parolee."

"Sheesh." Her eyes widened. "I sure can pick 'em, can't I?"

"That's why I keep telling you to let the police, FBI and

criminal investigators do their job." He shook her gently. "I can't leave you alone for a minute."

"I'm not a child to be babysat," she said, the indignation fading before the last word left her lips.

Being this close to Maggie stole the air from his lungs and made Joe want to pull her into his arms and take her there.

He leaned down and kissed her, driving his tongue between her teeth to duel with hers. When he drew back, she followed.

"I've missed this." He pressed his lips to her cheek and trailed a line of feather-soft kisses across her smooth skin to that erogenous zone behind her earlobe.

Tilting her head to the side to allow him better access to her ear, she muttered, "Me, too." She ran her hands up the back of his neck and pulled him down where she could nibble at his bottom lip.

There was only one place this kind of action would lead and Joe wasn't so sure he wanted to make love to Maggie in a smelly janitor's closet. He wanted her to know she was special, not a one-night stand to be taken advantage of in dark hallways or hiding places. Joe broke the kiss and held her at arm's length. "We should get out of here."

"Yes, we should," she replied softly. Her hands gripped his and she squeezed them. "Joe?"

"Yeah, baby?"

"Am I ever going to get my son back?"

THE SUN had set five hours earlier. Maggie paced the narrow aisles between the rows of empty desks at the tribal police station, chewing her fingernails to the nub and staring at the clock every five seconds. "Midnight! I don't think I'll make it to midnight," she grumbled, her heart aching to feel the warmth of her baby in her arms. She stopped for a moment in the middle of her pacing and squeezed her eyes shut. "Please, God, let him bring my baby to me."

A hand curved around her shoulders and pulled her back against a solid wall of muscles. The scent of mint and leather drifted into her senses, grounding her with the man she'd never stopped loving.

Joe.

"We'll get him back," he said.

"How do you know?" She spun and stared up into his face. All the waiting, worrying and frustration bubbled up in an explosion of nerves and anger. "Nobody's seen or heard him in all the searching that's gone on for the past three days. How the hell do you know he's not—" She gulped, swallowing the word before it could cross her lips, as if saying it would make it true.

Joe rested a hand on her shoulder. "Dakota is alive, Maggie. You have to believe that. And he'll need his mother to make things right when he comes home."

"I know." She leaned her forehead against his uniform shirt. "I know, but it's been three days. Will they have treated him right? Did they feed him and change his diapers?"

"He'll be fine." Joe pulled her into his arms and held her.

"The kidnappers said I had to go alone." She was scared and afraid they'd refuse to give Dakota to her.

"We'll be there."

"What if they know that?" Maggie stared up into his eyes as if she could predict the future in their dark-brown depths. "What if they don't let me have my baby because you're there?" She wanted Joe beside her, but if it meant not getting her baby back, then she'd rather go it alone.

"We have people moving into position around Coyote Butte as we speak. When it gets closer to time, you and I will go with the bag of meth."

The drugs. What all of this was about, the poison sold to kids on the reservation. And the ticket to the return of her son. "Is it the real thing?"

"No." Joe shook his head. "It's pretty well disguised so he shouldn't be able to tell."

"Are you sure? What if he can tell and refuses to give me my son?"

"That won't happen. We put a pretty good layer of the stuff around the outside of the bundle to give it the same look and feel."

"Nothing can go wrong with this trade tonight. I have to have my son. I need him and he needs me."

"I know." He hugged her again.

The warmth of his touch barely dispelled the chill settling in around her as the time neared.

"You ready?" he asked.

"Yes and no." Maggie pushed the hair behind her ear for the tenth time in the last two minutes, her hand shaking like a leaf in a storm.

Joe tipped her chin, forcing her to look up at him. "Do you want me to go instead?"

She shook her head. "The kidnapper told me to deliver it alone or they'd hurt Dakota. I can't risk it." She rested her hand on his sleeve. "Are you sure the others on the team won't be detected?"

"They'll be far enough back they won't be noticed. They have very strict instructions not to interfere."

"No snipers?" The thought of someone shooting in the dark made her stomach flip. "They might hit the baby."

"Everyone is under stand-down orders until I give them the word to move in."

Maggie breathed in, let it out and then glanced at the clock. "Okay. I'd better get going."

Joe handed her the package made up to look exactly like the methamphetamine. "I'll be watching from inside your car, so take the baby and get back into your car as soon as you make the trade."

Now that the time had come, she was oscillating between anticipation of getting her son back and complete terror of everything blowing up in her face. "What if they don't bring Dakota? What if this is all a setup?"

"We'll be there."

Setup or not, Maggie had to go, had to try to bring her son home. She squared her shoulders, tucked the package under her arm and faced Joe. "I'm ready."

He leaned close and kissed her. "You're a brave woman, Maggie. Paul would have been proud and Dakota will be too, when he's old enough to understand."

She snorted softly. "I don't feel so brave. My knees are shaking."

Joe wrapped an arm around her shoulder and walked her to the door of the office. The only person left in the building was the dispatcher who gave them a gentle smile and a thumbs-up.

Maggie needed a whole lot more than a thumbs-up to get her through this ordeal.

JOE SAT in silence in the passenger seat of Maggie's compact car for the trip out to Coyote Butte.

Maggie's fingers were white with the force of her grip on the steering wheel. He wished he could take all the worry from her and deliver her baby to her safe from harm. But the state criminal investigators and the FBI agent hadn't had any luck locating the child. It was as if he'd disappeared.

Joe hadn't given up hope. If this trade didn't take place tonight, he would personally search every last inch of the reservation until he found Maggie's child.

A mile out, Joe climbed into the back seat of the car and ducked low on the floorboard, tossing a black blanket over his entire body. If they were looking, they might see him, but they'd have to look really close. Between the tinted windows and the blanket, Joe felt nearly certain they wouldn't see him and harm the child.

He felt the car jerk to a halt.

"We're at the base of Coyote Butte," Maggie said. "I'm getting out."

"Be careful and be ready to drop to the ground in case of trouble."

"And that's supposed to make me feel better about getting out of the car?" she said, the pitch of her voice rising.

"Dakota's out there," he said.

"I'm going."

"Remember to leave the door ajar. I've set the lights so they won't come on."

"Okay. Here goes."

Joe waited for the sound of the door to open, but it didn't.

"Joe?"

"Yes, Maggie." He reached his hand around the side of the seat and touched her arm.

Maggie's hand clasped his fingers. "We still haven't had that talk."

"I know. But we will." And there was so much he wanted to say to this woman. "We will, later."

"But…" Maggie's fingers squeezed his once more then let go. "Yeah. We'll talk later."

The metallic sound of a door latch filled the air and the little car rocked slightly as Maggie got out. Joe held his breath, thinking Maggie might forget and close the door, but she didn't.

He could hear her boots crunch in the gravel, heading away from the car.

Maneuvering to peer out from under the blanket, he watched Maggie walk toward Coyote Butte. In her dark jacket, she was no more than an obscure silhouette against the darkness of the moonless night.

He tapped the headset perched on his ear, courtesy of Chase Metcalf and the FBI. "Del, are Metcalf and everyone else in position?"

"Roger," Del replied. "Awaiting your word."

"Roger. She's out of the car and moving toward the butte."

Maggie looked so alone, a small figure against the mountain of a task she had to accomplish. She stopped short of the butte and called out, "I have what you want. Where's my son?" Her voice echoed off the sheer rock surfaces, bouncing back several times before silence swallowed the words into the void.

Joe pulled his Glock out of his shoulder holster and

cocked it, all the while scanning the shadowy area below the rugged rise of land and rocks.

Silence reigned.

The skin on the back of Joe's neck tightened, and all the hairs stood out. The darkness loomed as if it were alive, lying in wait for something to happen.

Joe hated that he couldn't take the situation head-on, but the risks were too great. He could lose Maggie and her child if he didn't play it right.

The rattle of feet on loose gravel sounded close to the car and Joe ducked lower, his eyes at window level, his legs cramping in their tight position on the floorboard.

A dark figure moved in a crouch toward Maggie, carrying something that glinted in the meager light from the new moon. That something wasn't the shape, size or consistency of a baby.

All senses on alert, Joe climbed over the top of the seat and eased out onto the ground. If ever there was a time when it was necessary to move as quietly as his ancestors, it was now. He pressed his feet into the gravel, careful to tread flat-footed so as not to disturb the earth and rocks. To move in silence, he had to be completely aware of how his footsteps impacted the world around him.

Maggie stared up at the cliffs and shouted, "Where's my baby?"

Joe hurried behind the person sneaking up on Maggie, but he wouldn't reach her before the interloper did. Pure adrenaline rushed through his veins and he gave up on quiet and ran full-throttle toward them. "Look out, Maggie!"

Still ten yards out, Joe could only watch as the man plowed into Maggie like a lineman. He clipped her from behind with all the force of his headlong run, jerking the package from her hands. Then he disappeared into the shadows at the base of the cliffs.

Maggie spun in the gravel and fell backward onto the hard ground.

When Joe reached her, he knelt beside her. "Are you okay?"

"I'm fine," she said, struggling to rise. "But he got the package."

"Stay here. I'm going after him." Joe hit the button on his headset. "Move in!" Crouching low, Joe ran toward the base of the butte, zigzagging to avoid being an easy target.

The pop of gunfire echoed off the rocks, at the same time gravel spewed up in front of him, bouncing off his shins. Joe dove for the ground, rolled to the side and back onto his feet, resuming his race to catch the kidnapper.

When he reached the shadows, he worked his way slowly among the giant boulders that had fallen from the cliffs above. He forced his breathing to be quiet and his feet to rise and fall evenly as his father had taught him in the hunt. Quiet, like the mountain lion, moving with stealth and precision through the landscape, he became one with nature, blending with the dark.

Then he heard the distinct sound of a motor being kick-started. After the second kick, an engine roared to life and a four-wheeler spun out of the shadows three yards ahead and headed straight at him.

Joe braced his left hand under the Glock. He had a clear shot on the guy and he aimed for the man's chest. As he squeezed the trigger, the rider veered right and Joe's bullet missed. But the rider and his four-wheeler swerved back at Joe and clipped his left hip, sending him sprawling to the ground.

Rolling to his side, Joe shot off two more rounds, but the ATV and rider disappeared through the rocks, climbing up the side of the hill on a hidden path.

"Joe!" Maggie called out. "Joe!"

"I'm all right," he shouted. "For the love of Pete, get back to your car, now!"

Joe struggled to his feet and raced after the man and vehicle, picking his way through the rocks, cursing the throbbing in his hip and knees. He had to stop the guy and find out where Maggie's son was. When he found out he had a bad bag of drugs he'd be furious and just might take it out on the kid.

"Joe!" Maggie called out. "He's already over the top of the butte. You'll never catch him on foot."

Knowing she was right didn't make him slow until he knew without a doubt their kidnapper had gotten away. He turned and trudged back down the hillside as the rest of his crew raced in on foot and in vehicles.

"We missed him." Maggie stated the obvious. "And he got the fake drugs." She climbed into her car and sat with the door open, her face buried in her hands, rocking as if in a catatonic state. When she looked up at Joe, her face was drawn and a grayish-white in the limited light from the stars. "He didn't even bring Dakota. By the looks of it, he had no intention of bringing him." Tears welled in her eyes. "What am I going to do? How will I get him back, now?"

Chapter Thirteen

Joe's face looked like a stone statue of one of his ancestors, his jawline rigid and his eyes black and piercing. He stared down at her. "Del will drive you back to the station." He extended a hand and pulled her to her feet.

"No, I want to stay with you." She held tightly to his hand, afraid if she let go, her support would crumble.

"Just do it, Maggie. I'll meet you there as soon as I can." He dropped her hand and turned to Del. "I'll need the keys to your vehicle. Take Maggie back to the station and keep her there. I don't want her going anywhere else. Not home, not the center. She's to stay at the station until I return."

Anger built inside, pushing aside her previous disappointment and despair over the continued absence of her son. "You can't order me around like I'm one of your officers. I'm a citizen with rights."

He stared down at her, a twitch working in the muscles of his jaw. Then his face relaxed a little. "You're right. But I need to know you're safe so I can be free to do my job. Please, Maggie, go to the station with Del and wait for me." The look in his eyes was pleading. He needed to go after the man who had almost killed him. The man who knew the whereabouts of Maggie's son. She would only slow him down.

"Okay. I'll go." Her eyes narrowed into slits. "Get him, Officer Lonewolf," she said, her jaw set in determination. Then she rounded the front bumper to the passenger side of her car and got in.

Del tossed his keys to Joe. "Let me know if you need anything from our end."

"Roger." He laid a hand on Del's shoulder. "Take good care of her."

"You know I will." Del climbed into the driver's seat and started the engine.

Joe sprinted across to the SUV, shouting orders to the others pulling in around the base of the butte. He climbed in, spun the vehicle around and took off along the rutted road leading around the base of the hill. The other vehicles headed in the opposite direction.

"You think they'll find him?" Maggie asked.

"I doubt it. He's got the advantage being on a four-wheeler up there. He could be long gone before they reach the other side." Del backed in a half circle and headed back to town.

Craning her neck, Maggie watched as Joe's taillights disappeared around an outcropping of boulders. "You think he'll be all right?"

Del glanced in the rearview mirror. "Joe can take care of himself. He's been doing it since his father died when he was ten."

Maggie faced forward and settled in for the bumpy ride along the dirt road. "Joe was close to his father?"

"Yeah. He doesn't talk much about him, though. I remember when we were kids and his father used to take us on camping trips. Not only did he teach us how to identify different plants and animals, he taught us many of the values and beliefs of the Lakota. He was a good man and a good father to Joe."

That wad of guilt rolled over in Maggie's belly. Joe would be a good father to his son, if he ever got the chance.

Del drove on, a smile curving his lips. "Yeah, Joe's dad was real involved with the annual powwows and even had a program going to teach the kids the ancient Lakota ways. No one since has taught the old ways as well as Chaska Lonewolf. He learned the Lakota language from his grandparents and swore he'd see to it his son and grandsons would know it as well."

Dakota was Chaska Lonewolf's grandson. Would he grow up learning the ways of his forefathers? Maggie's breath caught in her throat.

She tried not to think it, but she couldn't help wondering whether or not Dakota would be given a chance to grow up.

JOE DROVE as fast as the terrain allowed without careening into house-sized boulders that had fallen from the walls of the butte. The longer it took to get around the massive natural obstruction, the more chance of the man on the ATV getting away. In his right mind, Joe would have given up. Going around the butte took twice as long as the ATV would take going up and over the top. He had about as much chance of catching up to the perpetrator as he did of winning Maggie back. There was little chance of a future with Maggie if the child died—Dakota's death would always be between them.

Joe had to try. If he didn't find him now, he'd be out here at the first sign of daylight combing the hillside for any shred of evidence that would lead to the arrest of a kidnapper and the recovery of one five-month-old baby.

Maggie had to be completely frantic by now. He wished he could be with her to help her through the long night, but he couldn't be in two places at once.

"Anything?" he asked into his headset, not even sure the radio waves would carry around or over the massive butte.

"Nothing yet," Metcalf said, his voice crackling but understandable.

If his calculations were correct, the ATV would make it to the road on the other side ten to fifteen minutes before either he or Metcalf's crew would. That would give the suspect time to lose himself in the canyon a mile from the north side of Coyote Butte.

Joe pressed his foot to the floor. He couldn't let that happen. Where was that road? He should be getting close. As he rounded a broad projection of fallen rocks and stumpy trees, something flashed in his headlights. He slammed on his brakes and backed his vehicle until he could see the shiny metal of handlebars crumpled against a boulder the size of his house. He touched his finger to the headset. "Got something here," he said into the mike.

"What is it?" Metcalf asked.

"A crashed ATV. Keep coming around until you see my headlights. I'm going to check it out."

"You want to wait for backup?"

"No." Joe pulled his SUV to a halt twenty yards away from the mangled ATV. He switched the engine off but left the headlights shining toward the crash site. If this had been the getaway ATV and Franks had been driving it when it hit the rock, the man wouldn't be in any condition to run very far.

Joe pulled the gun from his shoulder holster and his flashlight from beneath the seat. He emerged from the SUV, scanning the surrounding area and listening for any sign of movement.

Nothing stirred but the puffs of steam he exhaled into the cold night air.

Where was Franks? Or had it really been Bill Franks that had attacked him on the other side of the butte?

Joe slipped away from the protection of his vehicle and into the darkness outside the beam of headlights. He circled wide in case someone lay in wait ready to pop off a round or two while he bent over the mutilated ATV.

With one hand blocking the glare of the headlights and the other holding his pistol out in front, he searched the shadows, willing his eyes to adjust to the darkness. If someone was out here, they were very still. At gut level, Joe knew whoever had been here was either dead or gone.

As he approached the crash scene, Joe could make out a dark lump sprawled ten feet from the four-wheeler. At first he thought it was another pile of rocks until he moved closer. It wasn't a rock. The lines were too rounded. Rocks in these parts tended to be jagged.

Moving cautiously, he crouched next to a man's body lying face-down in the dirt. He reached out and touched a hand to his neck, feeling for a pulse but finding not even a trace. Shifting out of the path of the light from his vehicle, he could just make out Bill Franks's face. Or what was left of it after it had scraped across the jagged rocks. Blood soaked into the earth beneath Franks's body, more blood than a vehicle crash would produce. Joe shone his flashlight over the body and found a gunshot exit wound through Franks's back.

Someone had shot him as he maneuvered down the hillside. Someone who'd known he'd be there.

Joe widened the arc of his flashlight beam looking for the package of fake drugs.

Lights of an approaching vehicle appeared around the bend in the road and Chase Metcalf pulled up next to Joe's SUV and got out. "What did you find?" he called out.

"Franks."

Metcalf leaned into his vehicle and removed a camera. "Dead or alive?"

"Dead." Joe looked at Metcalf. "He was shot."

MAGGIE PACED the linoleum tiles between the desks in the tribal police station for the tenth time in the past two hours. "Why aren't they back yet?" She'd heard the radio calls and knew Bill Franks's body had been found. So what was keeping the rest of the team?

Del shook his head. "They have to mark the crime scene and collect what evidence they can before they can come back." The radio crackled on his shoulder and he reached for the mike. "Go ahead."

"This is Officer Lonewolf. I'm on my way in."

"Roger."

Maggie sighed and slipped into a chair behind a desk littered with manila file folders and stained paper coffee cups. At almost three o'clock in the morning, she was exhausted, but she couldn't dream of sleeping without hearing all the details of what had happened to Bill Franks. Plus, she wanted to see for herself that Joe was all right.

Her son's father needed to stick around long enough for her to tell him Dakota was his flesh and blood. As she recalled the sound of gunfire at the Butte, Maggie sucked in a deep, shaky breath. Joe had come close to being killed tonight and he still didn't know about the baby. For the past two hours, she'd berated herself as every kind of fool for keeping the information from him.

Maggie popped up from the chair and paced again. What was taking him so long?

"You know, pacing won't bring him in any faster." Del lounged back in a chair, his feet propped on the desk in front of him. With his cap pulled down over his eyes, he appeared to be sleeping, but the occasional comment thrown out into the silent room proved otherwise.

"I know. I can't help it."

"Have you told Joe about his son yet?" Del didn't look up from beneath the bill of his cap.

Maggie stopped in midstride and turned to stare at the tribal police officer who was one of Joe's best friends. "What?"

"You heard me." Del pushed the cap back and sat up, letting his feet drop to the floor with a thump.

"Does everyone on this reservation know Dakota is Joe's son, except Joe?" she asked.

Del tapped his fingertips on the desktop and stared at the far corner of the room before answering, "Maybe not everyone." His gaze returned to her and he smiled. "Just those who've done the math. Joe never was that good at math."

Maggie wrapped her arms around her middle and rocked back on her heels. "Every time I try to tell him, the timing just doesn't seem right."

"With the kid missing, no time is going to be right. He's likely to go ballistic."

"You think?" She pulled a chair in front of Del and sat. "Do you think he can ever forgive me for keeping it from him?"

"I don't know." He shook his head. "Family means a lot to Joe."

Maggie's teeth covered her bottom lip. "I should have told him."

"Unfortunately, you can't undo the past."

"No." But how she wished she could.

"So when *are* you going to tell him?"

"As soon as possible." Maggie sighed. Her decision was the right one, and she would tell him as soon as he got back. And as soon as she figured out how.

JOE STRODE into the police station, physically exhausted but mentally wired.

Del and Maggie jumped up from their chairs and crossed the room, meeting him halfway.

"What happened?" Maggie asked.

Joe wished the hell he knew. "Someone was waiting for Franks when he came down off the mountain."

"See any vehicles, tire tracks, anything?" Del crossed his arms over his chest.

"The ground was too dry and rocky around the base of the butte to get much of anything. Especially in the dark. We'll have a crew out there at daylight to collect more evidence."

"So we're back to square one?" Maggie's shoulders drooped as if the weight of the world rested on them.

"I'm afraid so." Joe ran a hand through his hair and down over his face.

"But who would have killed Franks? One of the Sukas? Randy Biko?" Maggie turned away and paced the long aisle through the row of desks. "Do you have any idea what it does to me knowing that whoever has my son is a murderer?" She stopped in the middle of the floor and slowly turned to face Joe. "Is that it? We have no leads, no idea who could have murdered Bill Franks, Bernie and maybe even Paul? Not to mention the little detail of kidnapping my son."

Joe felt her frustration, but he had nothing to offer that would ease her mind. "That about sums it up." He turned to Del. "I'll do the paperwork in the morning. I think I should get Maggie home for now."

"Roger. I'm headed that way myself. See ya in a few hours?"

"You bet." Joe could only hope the few hours would generate a miracle. Because they were going to need one to find Dakota now.

MAGGIE LED the way to her house with Joe following in his tribal police vehicle. She only went through the motions of going home. Her little cottage was anything but home without her baby.

After her outburst at the station, she'd clammed up. It wasn't Joe's fault they couldn't find the suspect and she couldn't think of anything that could make her feel better about the situation. So she kept her mouth shut and her thoughts to herself.

The facts were, her son was still missing and she had no light at the end of the tunnel. No ultimatum to fulfill, no trade pending. They'd blown it with the scheduled exchange. The kidnapper had gotten away with the fake drugs and until he figured out they were fake, she had nothing to bargain with.

Once inside, Joe made a sweep of the house to ensure no intruders lurked in the closets or under the bed.

At this point, Maggie couldn't care less. If someone came in and put a bullet through her heart, at least the pain would go away with her death.

She hovered in the doorway of her son's bedroom, staring into the shadows of what had once been a cheerful place. The crib stood silent against the wall as if the room had never held the joyous sounds of a baby cooing at the bright mobile that hung still above the bed.

Hands settled on her shoulders and turned her into arms so strong surely they could hold them both up through these sad times.

"You need to get some sleep. You look like death."

"Thanks, you know just what to say to a girl," she quipped, when all she felt like doing was crawling into her bed fully clothed and burying her head beneath her pillows.

Gentle hands eased her coat off her shoulders and he guided her into her bedroom, switching on the lights.

"Will I ever see my son again?" Maggie looked up into Joe's face.

"Yes, you will."

As she studied the lines beside his eyes, Maggie wondered if the time to tell him about Dakota was now. "Joe?"

"Yes, Maggie?" His hand reached out and tenderly tucked a strand of hair behind her ear. Then his fingers trailed along her cheek.

How could she think when he was being so nice? She brushed his hand away. "There's something you should know."

"I'm listening," He leaned over and pressed a kiss to her forehead. "Go ahead."

"About Dakota." She opened her mouth ready to blurt the whole story out, but at that exact moment, the telephone rang.

"It's three in the morning. Who would be calling?" Joe's jaw tightened. "Answer it, maybe it's the kidnapper."

Her heart pounded as she lifted the receiver and pressed it to her ear.

"If you don't give me what I want, both you and the baby will end up like Franks."

Maggie's hand shook so badly, she almost dropped the phone. "How do I know my son is all right?"

The voice didn't respond for several long seconds and then the sound of a baby crying came across the line.

"Dakota?" Maggie whispered.

"You have until tomorrow night to get me the device."

"You already have the drugs, what else could you want?"

"Paul stole it and I want it back."

"But I don't—"

"Tomorrow. Have it."

"Where? When?"

"I'll find you tomorrow."

"Oh, God, please let me have my son back." The line went dead. Maggie slid to the floor, dropping the phone from her nerveless fingers.

Joe sat on the carpet next to her and gathered her into his arms, rocking her as if she were the child.

"I heard Dakota. Oh, Joe, I heard my son." She turned her face into his chest, the tears falling unchecked.

"That's good." He lifted her chin and smiled down at her. "It means he's alive."

With her fingers clutching his shirt, she stared into his eyes. "You don't get it. He wants something Paul stole from him and I don't have any idea what it is. He said something about a device."

Joe held her cheeks between his palms. "What kind of device, Maggie?"

"I don't know. If I don't find it by tomorrow…" She couldn't finish the sentence. Instead she buried her face in the fabric of his shirt. "I can't lose Dakota."

"I know, baby. He's part of my family, too, and it burns me up to think of anyone hurting him."

Maggie nestled against Joe's chest, her eyes drooping, exhaustion claiming her, dragging her into a healing sleep. She didn't want to let go of Joe. Didn't want him to leave her again. "Hold me, Joe. I can't lose you, too."

Chapter Fourteen

Shortly after Maggie fell asleep against him, Joe moved her to the bed, removing her shoes and tucking her beneath the blankets. He settled beside her on top of the covers, not trusting himself to be close enough to touch, afraid he might take her into his arms and never let her go again.

Her bright auburn hair spilled over the white pillow, shining in the light from the nightstand. He hadn't bothered to turn it off, preferring to stare at the beautiful woman beside him while she was blissfully unaware. All his life he'd promised himself that he would marry Lakota. But Maggie had turned his world upside down and proven some promises should never have been made and were best broken.

Sometime in the early hours of morning, Joe drifted into a restless sleep, the call of his ancestors strong in his dreams. The more he strained to hear them, the less he understood.

As soon as the sun rose, he slid off the bed and left Maggie sleeping in the bedroom. Stopping in the kitchen, he wrote a brief note asking Maggie to call him when she woke and not to leave the house under any circumstance. She'd be better off searching every corner of the little cottage for the mysterious item Paul stole from the kidnapper.

Joe entered the police station after eight o'clock in the morning and was met at the door by Del and Agent Metcalf.

"We were just about to call you." Del held out a document. "I ran that scan on some of the casino employees who moved in recently from out of state. There's one in there you might find interesting. I've highlighted him."

Joe scanned the names marked with a yellow highlighter. "Murray Tyler." He glanced up at Del. "What was the charge?"

"Apparently, he was accused of embezzlement by the Lucky You Casino in Vegas, but all charges were dropped."

Where had he heard the name Lucky You Casino? Joe chewed on the name but his memory wasn't spitting it out. "Was there a reason why the casino dropped the charges?"

"No. But I bet we can get a warrant to search his books at the Grand Buffalo based on this."

"Paul worked with Murray at the Buffalo." Joe tapped his hand to the paper, regret a bitter taste in his mouth. He hadn't been there for his stepbrother when he was alive, but maybe he could help to save his brother's son. "Take this to Judge Sun Bear of the Painted Rock Tribal Court and get that warrant. Agent Metcalf, can you get an FBI agent experienced in embezzlement cases out here ASAP?"

Metcalf smiled. "Already on his way from Rapid City. Should be here within an hour."

"Then let's be ready when we get the warrant," Joe said. "I want all the information about the case that was dropped. Can you get your hands on that?"

"I've been going through what I could find online," the FBI agent said. "I'll call the court clerk and casino management for more details as soon as they get in. It's only seven o'clock their time."

"I'm headed out to Coyote Butte to see how the evidence-gathering is going. If Maggie calls, tell her I'll be back in an hour."

Del folded the printout and stuffed it in his inside jacket pocket. "Do I need to send a unit to keep an eye on her?"

"Just have someone drive by. I think she'll be okay during the daytime. She's going to go over the house inch by inch to see if she can find whatever it is the kidnapper says Paul stole from him."

"Not afraid she'll run off and get herself hurt?" Del asked.

"No. She's going to be busy searching for at least an hour. I'll check on her on my way back from Bill Franks's murder scene. She should be fine for an hour on her own."

"If you say so." Del shrugged. "I'm on my way over to Judge Sun Bear's house to get that warrant."

Joe left the building, pausing for a moment as the sun broke through the clouds that had smothered the prairie for the past week. After three days of dead ends and dead bodies, they were due a break in the weather and the case.

MAGGIE AWOKE when the sun poked through the cracks in her mini-blinds and urged her eyelids open. Even before she looked around, she knew she was alone. Joe had left while she slept.

A quick shower helped clear the sleep from her eyes and the fog from her brain. Once she'd tossed on jeans and a turtleneck sweater, she padded into the kitchen for a cup of coffee.

The note lay propped on the small dinette table, Joe's bold handwriting scrawled across the page. Maggie thought it funny how even his handwriting made her heart stutter.

She didn't need his note to tell her to search every inch of the house for whatever device Paul might have stolen. She'd planned on doing that anyway. If she had to rip every drawer, nook and cranny apart to find whatever it was, she'd do it. Her son's life depended on her finding the missing item.

She stared around the kitchen, desperation welling up in her chest. Tamping down the rising panic, she dove into the utensils drawer, examining every item in it as if it might be the magic key to her son's salvation.

Drawer after drawer, she tore everything apart, practically standing upside down to crawl inside the cabinets looking for anything unusual or maybe taped inside.

After an hour and a half, she found herself in Paul's room, up to her elbows in his clothing and personal items. Nothing stood out as worth trading a baby's life for.

When the panic and despair resurfaced, Maggie didn't try to stop it. Instead, she let it go in a long wailing moan.

How could the kidnapper expect her to find something if he didn't tell her what it was? And what kind of cruel game was he playing to hold her child's life over her head in order to retrieve it? What kind of monster would do such a thing?

The doorbell rang.

Maggie ignored it, settling into her misery with a vengeance. After the third ring, it dawned on her that maybe someone was there to bring back her son.

She leapt to her feet and raced for the door, yanking it open with such force the knob hit the wall, smashing a dent in the plaster.

Tracy Little Foot stood on the porch with wide, frightened eyes. "Maggie? Are you all right?"

For several seconds, Maggie struggled to remember how to breathe. Of course, the Lakota woman didn't have her son. Finally her lung function returned to normal and she managed to say, "I'm fine."

"For a moment there, you didn't look fine." Tracy didn't enter the house. "I can't stay. I just wanted to deliver this and to find out if you'd heard anything about Dakota."

"Dakota's still missing," Maggie said, her voice dull and flat.

"I'm so sorry to hear that. You must be out of your mind with worry. I hope they find him soon." Tracy held out a large envelope. "The postman delivered this yesterday while you were out. I'd stay and keep you company, but I'm late for work."

"It's okay. I understand." Maggie didn't want anyone staying with her as she wallowed in her misery. "Thanks, Tracy." She didn't wait for Tracy to leave, but shut the door and sank to the floor, her legs refusing to hold her up a second longer.

She wanted to cry, but she sat motionless, focusing on the playpen positioned in the far corner. Everywhere she'd searched she'd run across reminders of Dakota as if the toys, socks and pacifiers were each telling her to try harder.

Her gaze dropped to the envelope in her lap. It was from the Law Offices of Bradford, Taylor and Jones, Attorneys at Law in Rapid City. She'd never contacted an attorney in

Rapid City and she didn't recognize the name. Probably an ambulance chaser wanted her to sue someone for her husband's wrongful death. She'd received half a dozen such letters in the mail since Paul's death.

Tossing it aside, she pushed to her feet and wandered through the house, unable to think of a single place she hadn't looked. Where now? Her child's life depended on her finding the item.

She wished Joe were there to help. What would he do, if he'd looked everywhere? Who would he ask for guidance?

Matoskah.

The old tribal shaman. Of course! Whenever a Lakota was in trouble, he or she went to Matoskah for spiritual guidance.

Maggie grabbed her purse and keys and ran to her car. She'd been to visit the tribal elder right after Joe had left for Iraq. At the time, she'd been desperately unhappy and hadn't listened to what the old man had to say. He'd advised her to think about what she was doing and not make any rash decisions. She hadn't told him about the baby, but deep inside she had the feeling he knew.

Looking back, she wished she'd taken advantage of his wise words. Perhaps her son wouldn't be missing now if she had listened.

Perhaps he'd be able to help her find the missing article, or better still, find her son.

When she arrived at Matoskah's home, she wasn't surprised when Matoskah didn't answer the door. She'd been told by almost every member of the Painted Rock Tribe that the old shaman spent much of his day meditating in the sweat lodge. Rushing around the back of the house, she paused at the entrance to the hide-covered structure.

"Matoskah?" she called out, faintly uncertain of her welcome as a white woman.

"Enter the womb of the earth," said the deep melodious voice from within.

"ANY LUCK out there?" Del asked over the radio.

"Nothing worth mentioning." Joe glanced around at the South Dakota Division of Criminal Investigations team combing the ground for any trace evidence linked to Bill Franks's murder. "I was just about to head over to Maggie's. What's up?"

"We have the warrant, and Vince Jordan, the FBI agent from Rapid City, just rolled into the parking lot. Want to meet us at the Grand Buffalo?"

Joe hesitated. He hadn't seen Maggie in over an hour and a half. But the way she'd been sleeping when he left, she should have slept in. He glanced at his watch. Nine thirty-five. Perhaps she was just getting started at tearing through the house. "I'll meet you there." He'd call as soon as he got in range of the casino and cell phone reception to see if she'd come up with anything.

The thirty-minute drive across the prairie to the casino seemed to take forever when a baby's life was hanging in the balance.

When Joe stepped into the casino, he waited for his eyes to adjust from the brightness outside to the near-dark interior.

"Well, hello, Joe Lonewolf. Come slumming again?" Leotie Jones stepped in front of Joe on his way to the management offices, effectively blocking his path.

"I'm here on business, Leotie. Where's Gray?" He stepped around her and continued toward the back of the casino.

She fell in step and motioned to the side with her head, her black hair with brassy red streaks falling over her left cheek. "He's out to lunch. Del and that hunk of an FBI agent are in Murray's office doing something with his computer." Long, dark fingers tipped with blood-red nails flashed out to clutch his elbow, bringing him to a stop. "What's your hurry?"

His back teeth grinding together, Joe held on to his anger by a thin thread. "Not now, Leotie."

When he tried to pry her hand loose, her grip transferred to his fingers and she wouldn't let go. "You don't have time for an old friend?"

"No." He stared into her eyes, his mouth tight. Did she never give up? "Let go."

Ignoring his demand, she laced her fingers with his and smiled, looking up at him through long black lashes. "We used to be good together."

"We slept together once. A long time ago." Joe gripped her wrist and held her hand away from him. "There never was a 'we' and never will be."

"Because of her?" Leotie's smile turned into a snarl. "Are you still sleeping with Paul's widow?"

Paul's widow.

The way she put it hit Joe square in the gut. The guilt he'd felt since he'd slept with Maggie couldn't be shaken.

No matter how loveless his marriage, Paul hadn't been dead for three weeks yet.

Leotie must have sensed his hesitation or seen some of the remorse in his face. She moved closer, pressing her breasts to his chest. "You know she's been lying to you, don't you?"

"I don't want to hear this." He grabbed her shoulders and set her away. Then he turned and continued toward the rear of the building.

"Because you don't want to know the truth," she called after him. "She lied about her baby. She married Paul to hide her baby from the real father."

Joe's steps slowed, but he refused to turn around and acknowledge the crazy talk from a jealous woman.

"Don't you even want to know who the real father is?"

She had him.

Joe turned, his body moving slowly as if he were drugged. He didn't want to hear what she had to say but he couldn't help himself. "Why are you doing this, Leotie?"

She stood with her hands on her hips, her face set in a belligerent frown. "Because you should know the truth. That bitch lied to you."

He shouldn't be listening to her. Leotie was known for her mean streak and her gift for telling hurtful lies. "Go away." He stalked off in the direction of the offices.

"She didn't tell you because she didn't want you to know. Joe," Leotie shouted. "Dakota is your son."

Chapter Fifteen

Her head still floating in the cloud of steam from the sweat lodge, Maggie returned to her little cottage. Although Matoskah hadn't told her anything she didn't already know, she felt as if the visit to the old shaman wasn't a waste of time.

"Look where you haven't. Open your thoughts and mind to everything and the answer will come."

After parking in the driveway, she climbed out of the car and stood in the frigid air. A cold northwestern wind blew across the prairie finding its way beneath the warm wool jacket she wore. She pulled her collar up to her chin and stared at the house. Where hadn't she looked? Outside?

Despite the freezing temperature and sub-zero wind-chill factor, Maggie scoured the exterior of the house, turning over stones, the flowerpot with the dead geranium and the welcome mat on the front porch. She skimmed her fingers along the tops of the forest-green shutters. Nothing. With her teeth chattering so hard in her head that she couldn't hear herself think, Maggie unlocked the door and stepped into the warmth inside.

The big envelope still lay on the floor where she'd left

it and she bent to retrieve it. As she leaned over, her purse dropped off her shoulder and onto the floor, all its contents spilling out on the carpet.

"Damn." As she scooped the items back in her purse, she stared at the envelope, Matoskah's words echoed in her head.

Open your thoughts and mind to everything.

Might as well start here. Her fingers still stiff from the cold, Maggie stripped her gloves from her hands and struggled to rip the large envelope open. Inside was a business letter with the law firm's header at the top and a message from Giles Taylor.

"It is with deep sympathy—"

Maggie collapsed in the wooden rocking chair beside her, not sure she was up to reading another condolence, but determined to deal with it and set it aside. She continued to read.

"—we send this letter at the bequest of your late husband, Paul Eliot Brandt. In the event of his untimely death, he instructed this law office to send the enclosed envelope to you to dispose of as you see fit."

Maggie's heart caught in her throat as she thought of Paul lying peacefully in his casket, looking as if he'd gone to sleep in the middle of a funeral. He'd been so young to be dead. At this time of his life he should have been happily married with several children of his own. He'd deserved a wife who could love him. Instead he'd married Maggie and given up on his chance at happiness.

Now Paul was dead.

She lifted the unopened envelope and weighed it in her hand. What did he leave for his wife-in-name-only? He hadn't had a will and the life insurance policy he'd had through the casino was barely enough to see her and Dakota through the next year.

Tearing at the seal, she ripped open the letter and removed a single white sheet of paper with the words Rapid City Bank & Trust written in Paul's boxy letters and a key taped to the center.

Why would Paul send her a key?

She removed the shiny brass key from the tape and held it in her hand. Was this the item the kidnapper had been so adamant about retrieving?

Maggie climbed to her feet, her blood surging through her veins.

Or was the item stored in a safe deposit box at the Rapid City Bank & Trust?

Slinging her purse over her shoulder, she raced out the door, not even bothering to lock it behind her. This could be the break she'd been looking for. Whatever this key belonged to could hold the answer to the mystery item Paul had supposedly stolen from the kidnapper.

DAKOTA WAS his son?

Joe stood in a daze outside Murray Tyler's office with Del, Metcalf and Vince Jordan as they waited for Gray Running Fox to show up.

"You okay, Joe?" Del asked.

Joe turned to look at Del without actually focusing on his friend. "What?"

"I asked if you were okay?" Del frowned. "You look a little pale. You're not catching something, are you?"

Running a hand over his short-cropped hair, Joe answered, "No. I'm fine." But was he?

If Leotie was right, he was a father.

Though his mind had a hard time wrapping around the revelation, all the pieces fell into place and Joe had to admit it could be true.

He'd left for Iraq fourteen months ago. Dakota was five months old. The night of the drug raid at the center had been a week before he shipped out.

"What's going on here?" Gray Running Fox strode down the corridor to the accountant's office, his face set in an angry scowl.

Del handed him the warrant. "Seems Murray Tyler has a reputation for skimming the books at casinos. The tribal council authorized a complete audit of the Grand Buffalo's accounting records."

Gray scanned the document and then shook it. "This is crazy."

"Look, Gray," Joe said. "The council is concerned that Murray's references and employment history weren't screened sufficiently. They have the right to conduct an audit at any time they choose in the interest of the tribe. We're taking Murray's CPU and all of his accounting data."

"What?" Gray's face paled beneath his dark complexion. "Why wasn't I given notice? We need to conduct backups to ensure the continued support of our operation."

"Sorry. We're taking it. And while these guys collect the information, maybe you can explain how someone convicted of embezzlement was hired on the staff here?"

"Murray was never convicted of embezzlement. I checked his record myself. The charges were dropped."

"If you'd unlock the door, we can get on with the audit and get through this as soon as possible."

He unlocked the door. "I'm calling Judge Sun Bear."

"Go for it." Del tapped the paper in Gray's hand. "He signed the warrant. It's all in the document. The Painted Rock Tribal Council authorized the FBI to conduct a thorough review of the accounting records to ensure there are no discrepancies. I'm sure there's nothing to worry about if your books are straight."

Vince, Del and Metcalf entered the office while Joe and Gray stood outside the door.

"But I need my records to update with the daily receipts."

"Guess you'll have to make do without," Del said as he unplugged the monitor and keyboard from the back of the computer.

"This is crazy." Gray moved out of the way as Vince carried Murray's CPU out of the office and down the corridor. "How am I supposed to run the casino without the accounts?"

"What do you do when the computers aren't working?" Joe asked. "And can you tell me where Murray is? We'd like to ask him a few questions."

"He's probably still at home. He doesn't usually come in until after two o'clock."

While Del and Agent Metcalf completed loading files and disks into a box and followed Vince down the hallway, Joe nodded at Gray. "We'll be in touch. If I were you, I wouldn't go far. Let's hope your Mr. Tyler doesn't have anything to hide. But if he does, we'll find it. Thank you for your cooperation."

Joe left Gray standing in the hallway and walked away. By the time he reached the exit door, he was struggling to breathe and welcomed the cool blast of artic breeze in his face.

Del stood next to his police SUV, staring after a low-slung silver Saab blasting out of the parking lot. "That Leotie sure has a burr under her saddle."

"That's one angry woman," Metcalf commented, a smile lifting the corners of his mouth. "Looks like a new car."

"She said she hit a deer three weeks ago."

The FBI agent shook his head. "The way she drives, I'm not surprised. The deer don't have a chance."

Del and Agent Metcalf's conversation flowed over and around Joe with nothing sticking or taking root. So much had changed in the past three weeks. Paul's accident, Bernie and Tom getting shot, and now he'd learned he had a kid.

Del shot a look at Joe. "What gives?"

"Nothing." *Everything. I'm a father.* Joe almost wished he'd never bumped into Leotie Jones or heard about his son. All of a sudden he couldn't form a coherent thought to save his life.

Vince Jordan settled the CPU in the back of the SUV and closed the hatch. "Let's do it."

"See you back at the office," Del called out from his vehicle. "And, Joe, if you need anything, call."

Nodding, Joe climbed into his vehicle. He had a detour to make before he went back to the office. A detour for a little personal information-gathering with one red-haired social worker.

Balancing his cell phone in his hand, Joe thought about calling Maggie. Before Leotie had dropped her bomb on him, he'd planned to call her and check to make sure she was all right. Now he couldn't force his fingers to punch the necessary buttons into his phone.

What would he say? *Hi, this is the father of your child.*

Joe pounded his fist against the steering wheel, welcoming the pain that reminded him how stupid he'd been.

For over a year, Maggie had known but had chosen not to tell him about his son. Since he'd returned from Iraq, he could have been getting to know Dakota and been a part of his life, watching him grow.

Now his son was being held hostage to trade for some unknown object.

His five-month-old son.

Joe rested his forehead against knuckles wrapped so tightly around the steering wheel his fingers were white with the strain. How could he have been so blind? All this time, he'd been willing to do anything for Maggie, even dreaming up ways to woo her back. He'd asked for her forgiveness for turning her away.

Was that it?

Joe groaned as he turned the key in the ignition. She'd hidden the truth because he didn't want her to be a part of his Lakota life. How could he expect her to trust him with her child when he hadn't trusted her with his heart?

Anger and disappointment bubbled near the surface over all the time he'd lost getting to know his son. The anger was tempered by the realization that he'd more than set the stage for Maggie's deception.

He couldn't put off the meeting any longer. He had to see Maggie, had to hear her reasons. After a deep breath, he set the shift in Drive and pulled out of the casino parking lot and onto the main road leading back to the town of Buffalo Bluff.

In his head, he tried to think of the words he'd use to question Maggie. His first instinct was to blurt it out. Let her know what a terrible thing she'd done.

Then he remembered the different times over the past few days she'd tried to tell him something, only to be interrupted. Had she been trying to tell him about Dakota?

When he pulled up outside her house, the first thing he noticed was that there was no car in the driveway. When he'd left her that morning, her little red compact car had still been there.

Alarm bells rang in his brain. He should have had Del assign a unit to watch over her.

Jumping out of his SUV, he ran to the door to check inside, not that he had a key.

His heart flipped over in his chest when the handle turned and the door swung open. She hadn't locked it? Had she left of her own accord, or had she been forced out by the kidnapper?

All his anger morphed into a sudden petrifying fear for Maggie. Joe raced through the house, noting the overturned dresser drawers and the contents of cabinets strewn over the floor of the kitchen and bathroom. Had she been responsible for the disarray, or had someone gone systematically over every inch of the house?

Where was Maggie?

Yanking his cell phone out of the clip on his belt, he dialed her number and waited for her to answer. On the fourth ring, her answering machine picked up.

"This is Maggie, leave a message at the beep."

Why wasn't she answering? Was she in trouble or out of range? Out of range was highly likely in the middle of the prairie—cell reception being sporadic at best.

When the phone beeped, he said, "This is Joe, call me."

Part of him wanted to mention the baby, but his main

concern at this particular time was knowing Maggie was safe and not at the mercy of the kidnapper. They could work through their issues when Maggie was back at home with Dakota. In the meantime, Joe had a job to do.

ON THE WAY into Rapid City, Maggie dialed information for the phone number to the Rapid City Bank & Trust. Once connected, she asked for directions. She couldn't afford to waste time wandering around the city looking for the right bank and the right branch. She had to get to that safe deposit box, retrieve whatever was in it and get back to the reservation in case the kidnapper called or tried to find her.

She hoped that this was the item Paul had stolen. Maggie was certain nothing in that box was worth losing her son over. She'd trade her soul for her son's safe return.

When she finally pulled up outside the bank, she shifted into Park and peeled her fingers off the steering wheel, realizing for the first time how tightly she'd gripped it for the past hour on the road.

She drew in a shaky breath and climbed out of the car. This had to be it. It just had to.

Inside the bank she asked the petite blond clerk at the information desk where the safe deposit boxes were.

"If you'll wait just a moment, I'll have our vault manager assist you." The blonde punched a button on the phone beside her. "Mr. Deaton, you have someone wishing to access her safe deposit box."

Maggie paced in front of the desk until a small man dressed in a gray suit appeared. "May I help you?"

Holding up her key, Maggie asked. "I'd like to get into my safe deposit box, please."

After checking her full name against his database and making a copy of her driver's license, the man showed her into a vault where hundreds of little metal doors lined the walls. She then located the number corresponding to the number on the key.

Holding her breath, she turned the key in the lock and the box slid open. Inside were what looked like two computer memory-storage devices, like the one Paul used to carry around on his key chain. He'd called them memory sticks.

What were they doing in here, and what did they contain that was important enough to kill three men for and kidnap a baby?

Maggie lifted one of the memory sticks out of the box and weighed it in her hand. For such a small and insignificant piece of plastic and metal, someone wanted it really badly.

She lifted the other. Written on it in black marker was the word *copy.* She set it back in the deposit box as insurance in case she lost or destroyed the other. Then she tucked the other into her pocket, pushed the drawer closed and pulled out the key.

The little data-storage device had cost three people's lives and it felt as though it was burning a hole in her pocket. Whatever it contained must be damaging to someone.

She had to get the memory stick back to the reservation and into the hands of the tribal police and FBI. The sooner the better. Time seemed to be running out. If she wanted her baby back alive, she needed to know what was on the storage device and why it was so important.

Chapter Sixteen

Joe pressed the mike on his radio. "Del?"

"Yeah, boss. Where are you? We thought you were right behind us?"

"I made a detour," Joe said. "Are you at the station?"

"Yeah, got here ten minutes ago. Vince has the CPU powered up and he's going through the files as we speak."

"Good." Joe exhaled deeply. "Del, have you seen Maggie?"

"Not since yesterday. I thought you said she'd be at home trying to find whatever it is the kidnappers want."

"I just left her house. She's not there, her car is gone and her door was unlocked."

The radio was silent for a few seconds longer than normal, and then Del's voice came through. "I'll notify the force to keep a lookout for her."

"Thanks." Joe couldn't stop the rising panic churning through him. He should never have left Maggie alone, especially knowing how impetuous she was. A woman desperate to find her baby who was willing to follow a gang member out into a deserted canyon couldn't be trusted to make rational decisions when it came to protecting her own life. "I'll be there in five."

Joe strode into the station in just under five minutes. "Anything on Maggie?"

"No. The unit swung by there forty-five minutes ago and her car was still there. Nobody else has seen her since we put out the APB."

Joe muttered a curse beneath his breath. Where was she?

Del continued. "Found something interesting in Murray's files. There's an entire database that was sent to the Recycle Bin a month ago, just before Paul's death. Only we can't get it to come up or open."

Vince looked up from the monitor he'd hooked to the CPU. "From what I can make out, our friend Murray is tucking away some funds in bogus accounts."

Del let out a low whistle. "Surprise, surprise."

Joe had never liked the idea of a casino on the reservation, having heard of the problems they created. But he'd seen what the money could provide for his people in the form of a new hospital, educational opportunities and drug and alcohol rehabilitation programs. To think someone was siphoning that money into his own pocket burned Joe's insides.

"Think it's time to bring in Tyler and Gray Running Fox for questioning?" Del asked.

"Bring 'em in," Joe said, his mind shifting to Maggie's disappearance, the money pilfering at the casino a distant second in priority. He flipped his cell phone open and speed-dialed her number. After only one ring, it switched to her voice mail. Why didn't she answer?

As he stared at the cell phone, it rang and he almost

dropped it. The number in the display window wasn't Maggie's. "This is Joe."

"Joe, this is Tom Little Elk."

With all that had been going on in the past few days, he'd almost forgotten Tom lying in the hospital. "How are you, Tom?"

"I'd be much better if the damned doctors would let me go home to my own bed," Tom grumbled. "But that's not why I called. Do you have a minute? Can you come by to see me? I wanted to tell you something, but not over the phone."

"I'll be there." Joe flipped his phone shut. "I'll be out of the station for a few minutes. Call me if you hear anything from Maggie."

"Roger," Del said as he stood behind the FBI agent, his gaze glued to the monitor.

At the hospital, Joe nodded at the police guard and walked through the doorway into Tom's room.

Winona moved from beside the bed, her eyes glowing. "Tom's going to be just fine. He's grumpy as a grizzly because the doctor hasn't been by with the release papers, but he'll live."

Tom reached out and squeezed Winona's hand. "Mind if I have a word with Joe?"

Winona smiled brightly. "Of course I don't mind."

When she didn't move to leave, Tom added, "Alone?"

Her lips rounding into an *O*, Winona nodded. "Alone. Of course. I'll just go to the cafeteria for a cup of coffee."

"Thank you," he said, squeezing her hand once more before he let go.

As soon as Winona left the room, Joe moved to Tom's bedside. "What's up, Tom?"

"I was hoping you could tell me?" Sitting with his bed in the up position, Tom eased higher against the pillows.

"What do you mean?"

"When the shooting first occurred, I didn't see it coming. It wasn't until I woke up in the hospital that I heard about poor Bernie."

Joe nodded, but didn't interrupt.

"Bernie had his problems, but he wouldn't have committed suicide. Hell, he's been down on his luck before and pulled through. And Bernie wasn't mad at me for taking him out of the casino. In fact, he and I were laughing when we left. No way Bernie shot me."

"I figured that. Bernie didn't commit suicide because the gun was in his right hand."

Tom's eyes rounded. "Bernie's left-handed!"

"Right," Joe said. "Go on with your story."

"Once they quit doping me up for the pain, I got to thinking about what happened that night that might make someone want to kill Bernie and me." Tom paused.

"And?"

"When we left the casino, we were walking out to our cars. I saw Gray Running Fox handing an envelope over to that guy from the National Indian Gaming Commission. I didn't think anything of it until I ended up here."

"You sure you didn't see anything else?"

"Nothing. We went out the side door. You know the one the office staff uses. Hardly any of the customers use that door or that side of the parking area. It was just Bernie, me, Gray and that NIGC guy."

Joe stood. "Thanks, Tom."

"I don't want to get anyone in trouble for anything they didn't do, but if this helps get Maggie's baby back…"

"You've been a big help. If I were you, I'd stay another day until we get this case settled. The officer outside will make sure you stay safe."

"Think they'll come back to finish the job?"

"Not if we can help it," Joe said.

AT NINETY MILES AN HOUR, the little red car's four-cylinder engine was screaming. Maggie didn't care if she blew up the engine, as long as she got back to the police station with the memory stick in less than an hour.

As she made the turn to enter the reservation, she barely slowed, fishtailing on loose gravel. If the tribal police stopped her for speeding, she'd just have them take her the rest of the way in with the lights on.

The road stretched out in front of her and she still had another ten miles to go when she saw the shiny silver car parked on the side of the road. Cars broke down a lot on the reservation and were abandoned on the side of the road until someone could get there to tow them away. But this was a new car and it wasn't completely off the road.

Frustrated by the delay, Maggie slowed and peered into the parked car to see if someone needed assistance.

Just as she pulled alongside the vehicle, the car jerked out into the road, broadsiding Maggie's smaller car. As she careened off the road and onto the hard, dry prairie, she caught a glimpse of Leotie Jones, a vicious scowl on her face.

Maggie struggled to keep her car from spinning out of control, thankful the ground was fairly flat and that very little vegetation blocked her. However, in order to get to the police station in Buffalo Bluff, she had to get back on the road.

Pressing her foot to the accelerator, she lurched up onto the road only to be hit again and sent sliding off into the ditch.

Anger boiled up inside her. Leotie had been the one with the upper hand up until now. But Maggie was through playing nice.

Swerving back up onto the road, she aimed for the driver's door and the woman inside, hitting the vehicle at almost a ninety-degree angle. The silver Saab slid sideways off the road and flipped over once before it landed on its wheels.

Maggie slammed on her brakes and screeched to a halt, sitting crossways in the middle of the road and breathing hard from fear and adrenaline.

Other than the crumpled roof, Leotie's car sat in the ditch looking as if it was supposed to be there. The engine had cut off and Leotie slumped behind the wheel rubbing her forehead where a purple bruise was beginning to show.

Still riding her anger, Maggie jumped out of the car and ran to Leotie's, yanking open her door. "What the hell do you think you were doing?"

Leotie pressed her hand to her forehead again and then glared up at Maggie. "Don't you know anything? Are you that stupid you couldn't figure it out?"

"Is this about Joe?"

"Of course it's about Joe."

"You'd *kill* me to get Joe?" Maggie backed away in shock.

"Yes! If that's what it takes. I'd kill your kid, too!"

Her statement blasted through Maggie's brain and she reached in and grabbed Leotie by the shirt, dragging her out of the car with a strength she didn't know she had. "What do you know about my baby?"

Leotie shoved Maggie's hands away. "Nothing."

She was lying.

Maggie grabbed her again and thrust her against the hood of the crumpled silver Saab. "You'd better start talking, or I swear to God, I'll pull you apart one limb at a time."

Leotie stared into Maggie's hard gaze and must have seen the truth, because her own eyes widened and she shrank back against the vehicle. "You won't hurt me."

"Watch me." Maggie pulled her close and shoved her back against the car so hard Leotie's teeth rattled. "You got something you want to tell me or are you going for more of the same?"

"I have nothing to say," Leotie gasped.

Maggie slammed her against the car again. "Tell me!"

"Okay, okay." Leotie's shoulders slumped. "I stole your baby."

"You what?" Maggie lifted the woman by the collar of her jacket, anger and shock filling her veins with adrenaline. She'd never suspected Leotie of taking Dakota.

"I stole your baby." she said it with a defiant sneer even though Maggie had her by the collar.

She banged Leotie against her car again, tears of anger building behind her eyelids. "Why?"

"We needed a bargaining chip and your son was it." Leotie's hands rose up and slapped Maggie's aside. Then she dove into her driver's seat, slamming the door.

Before Leotie could turn the key, Maggie yanked the door open again. The Lakota woman twisted the key in the ignition, but the car didn't start. "Damn!" She slammed her palm against the steering wheel.

Maggie leaned in the doorway and ripped the keys from the ignition. "'We' who?"

"I don't have to tell you anything." The woman stared up at her with cold, uncaring eyes.

Fighting the urge to slap the sneer off Leotie's face, Maggie forced her voice into calmness. "You're in too deep now. You might as well come clean. Because if you don't tell me what this is all about and where my son is, I promise you this—I'll beat it out of you."

Leotie stared out the cracked windshield, tears filling her brown eyes. "I wanted Joe." Her head dropped forward onto her hands. "I've always wanted Joe."

Maggie already knew how much Leotie wanted the man and she could understand the woman's obsession. Wasn't she equally obsessed with Joe?

Her body stiffened. The difference being, she would never steal another woman's baby. "Were you the one who threw the rock through the window that night?" The night she'd made love to Joe.

"Yeah. And I wish it had hit you in the head," Leotie said, her voice a vicious growl.

"What does your jealousy over me and Joe have to do with you taking my son?"

Leotie slammed her hand against the steering wheel. "Because Joe's the father!"

Maggie shook her head. "Does everyone know about my baby but Joe?"

Leotie's mouth turned up on one side in a smirk. "Oh, Joe knows, all right."

Maggie barely resisted the urge to grab the woman by the throat. "How?"

"I told him this morning at the casino." Leotie laughed, the sound anything but joyful. "He was really pissed."

Maggie's heart banged against her ribcage. "Get out."

"Are you going to slam me against the car again?" Leotie asked. "Because, if you are, I'm staying right here."

"No. I just want to look in your eyes as you tell me why you've done this to me and my child."

Leotie eased from the car and stood with her arms crossed over her chest. "What do you want me to say?"

Maggie closed the car door and planted her fists on her hips, more to keep from reaching out to strangle the woman for telling Joe something Maggie should have told him long ago. She had no one to blame but herself. But that didn't take the steam out of her. No, this woman had taken her child.

Joe's anger would have to wait. She'd figure out how to explain later. What Maggie needed now was her son. "Where's Dakota?"

"At my father's old hunting cabin."

Braced to shake it out of Leotie, Maggie was shocked that the woman had given her such a quick response. "How is he? Who's taking care of him?" Many questions bubbled up but she stopped and waited for Leotie's answer.

"The kid's fine. My mother's taking care of him."

Was she lying?

"Where's your father's hunting cabin?"

"In the hills close to Eagle's Nest Bluff." Leotie stared down at her fingernails. "Damn, I broke a nail."

Maggie wanted to slap the woman's hand and make her

pay attention. "How did you think you could get Joe by stealing my baby? And what's the trade?"

"After Paul's death, I knew Joe would come sniffing around you again. If he knew about his kid, he'd be really mad, but he'd eventually forgive you and want to raise him with you as one happy little family." She stared up at Maggie, her eyes narrowed into slits. "I wasn't going to let that happen."

"So you stole my baby?"

"Yeah. It was easy. My mother used to rent your cottage. I had a key. I went in during the day and left a window unlocked. You really should be more careful you know."

"You bitch."

"I planned to drop the kid at an adoption agency as soon as the heat died down, but then the guys found out I had the baby—"

"What guys?" Maggie demanded.

Leotie glanced around as if afraid to bring it up. "I can't tell you. They'll kill me if they know I told you."

Her attempt to act afraid wasn't convincing Maggie. Not after all she'd done. Leotie was in up to her eyeballs on this deal. "Is that where the trade comes in?"

"Yeah, apparently Paul stole some information from them in the form of a database or something. One of them got mad and ran him off the road. Now they don't know where that database is. Do you?"

So that was what was on the memory stick. "And they're afraid of it getting into the wrong hands?" Maggie's eyes narrowed. "Why?"

"I told you, I can't tell you because they might kill me."

"And you're more afraid of them than me?" Maggie

stepped closer. "You kidnapped my baby. If I were you, I'd be afraid."

Leotie snorted and ran a quick gaze from the top of Maggie's head to her toes. "As far as I know, you haven't put a bullet in anyone."

"Yet." Maggie emphasized the *T*.

Leotie's smirk faded. "Look, I don't want to be part of this anymore. If you can get those guys off my back, you can have your kid back. Deal?"

"You're in no position to deal, Leotie. You're going to take me to my son and then you're going to tell the police everything you know."

Leotie crossed her arms over her chest. "Why should I?"

"Because if you don't, I'll take you out myself." Maggie grabbed the woman by the arm and shoved her toward the passenger side of her compact car, angry enough to follow through on her threat. "Now, get in."

Leotie shrugged. "Whatever. I'm tired of that brat, anyway."

Maggie climbed behind the wheel and stuck her key in the ignition. After three and a half long days, she was going to get her baby back. And when she did, she'd find a way to make it right with Joe.

Chapter Seventeen

On his way out of the hospital parking lot, Joe forced himself to turn toward the police station, resisting the urge to swing by Maggie's house. The radio on his shoulder squawked.

"Joe, Maggie just called," Del said.

His foot jerked off the accelerator and a hundred thoughts raced through his head at once. "Where is she?"

"She called on her cell phone and the signal wasn't great. The best I could make of it was she's on her way out to Eagle's Nest Bluff."

"What the hell for?" Here she goes again, Joe thought. Maggie was going to conquer the world all by herself. She sure made it hard for him to rescue her.

"She's got Leotie with her. And Joe, they're on their way out to get the kid."

His son. "They found Dakota?" The name felt awkward on his tongue, like that of a stranger. His son was a stranger to him.

Del cleared his throat. "Before the signal broke up, Maggie said what sounded like Leotie was the one who took him."

Leotie? Why hadn't he suspected the woman? She hated

everything to do with Maggie. And she would know that stealing her child was the worst thing she could do to a young mother.

He should have known. "You say Maggie had Leotie *with* her?"

"Yeah." Del's answer was short. He knew Leotie and how manipulative she could be. She'd talked the tribal court out of punishing her for possession when she had been undeniably guilty.

"Damn." Joe had no doubt in his mind Maggie could handle Leotie. When it came to Dakota, she'd attack an angry mountain lion to save her son. A smile twitched at his lips. "What about Gray and Murray?"

"I sent a unit out to the casino to get them. Neither one was there. The units are on the way to their homes as we speak."

"Del, when Maggie talked to the kidnapper on the phone, she referred to him as a 'he.' Leotie could be leading her into a trap. Get out to Eagle's Nest Bluff now."

"Where could they have kept a baby out there for the past three nights?" Del asked.

What was out there? Joe slowed to turn onto the main road leading out of town and toward Eagle's Nest Bluff. "Isn't there an old hunting cabin in the hills around the bluff?"

"That old trapper's cabin?" Del asked. "I thought it had fallen down."

"Maybe it hasn't." His father had taken him there when he was eight years old. Twenty-three years ago it had looked as though it could be blown over in a stiff northwestern breeze. But that was the only structure he could think of. He hoped to hell he could find it on the twisting paths through the hills. "I'll be out there before you. Make sure you bring reinforcements." He paused and then said, "Hey Del, be careful. These guys play for keeps."

As images of Paul, Bernie and Bill Franks flashed through his memory, Joe's booted foot pressed hard to the floorboard.

His SUV shot through the paved streets of the reservation and out toward the eastern hills. The sun shone in his rearview mirror, a bright blob of orange spreading along the gray and yellow prairie as if melting into the horizon. If he didn't hurry, the sun would disappear from the sky, and he might miss the turnoffs altogether.

He couldn't get lost on the prairie. Not now. Not when Maggie and Dakota needed him.

Halfway out to the bluffs, his radio squawked again. "Joe, we found Murray."

"Is he talking?"

"Not much. He's dead."

Had Gray gone over to Murray's after they'd left the casino? Was he already out at Eagle's Nest Bluff waiting for Maggie and Leotie to show up? Joe's stomach lurched.

If Gray had killed Murray, he'd be on his way out to get his bargaining chip. Dakota. He could run all the way to Mexico using the child as collateral.

Fear squeezed Joe's lungs until he struggled to breathe. Maggie had a good head start on him and he hadn't seen Gray in several hours. The casino manager had had plenty of time to kill a man and get to the bluff ahead of Maggie and Leotie.

MAGGIE KEPT one eye on the road and the other on Leotie for the entire drive out to Eagle's Nest Bluff. She wasn't naive enough to trust the woman for a minute. The farther out on the prairie they went, the more her gut told her that this could be a trap and she'd been stupid not to go with backup. She didn't even own a gun.

She glanced down at her cell phone hoping for a miracle and a few green bars indicating reception in this cell phone-challenged corner of the world. Cell phones were notoriously useless on the reservation once out of town. The call she'd placed to the tribal police had had sketchy reception at best. *Please let them know where to look.*

She could kick herself for not going straight to the police station with Leotie and letting them bring her out to the bluff to find her baby.

Again, her instinct told her time was important if she wanted to see Dakota alive.

"Who's taking care of Dakota?" Maggie asked.

"What's it matter? He's being taken care of."

Maggie slowed, shooting a venomous look toward Leotie. "Don't push me."

"Chill, woman. I told you my mother's watching him." Leotie's eyes rolled upward and she crossed her arms over her chest.

Maggie fought the sarcastic remark that rose to her lips. Based on Leotie's current attitude and reputation, that didn't say much for her mother. But having been a social worker for five years, Maggie knew parents weren't the only factor in a person's mental state. Peers, environment and chemical balance played as big a role in behavior. She prayed Leotie was one of the cases where the mother wasn't at the root of Leotie's personality disorders.

She wanted to pump Leotie for answers to all her concerns over her son's well-being, but she held her tongue. She knew how mean and spiteful the woman could be and didn't want to open herself to more heartache at the hands of this monster who'd stolen her son from his bed. Her anger simmered beneath a thin layer of control. If she wasn't so afraid for her son, she'd be tempted to beat the hell out of Leotie for what she'd done.

The sun had dropped low in the sky and would soon disappear below the horizon and she hadn't seen so much as a house, hut or cave for the past twenty minutes. Maggie was just beginning to think Leotie was leading her on a wild-goose chase when the woman in question pointed to a dirt trail several yards ahead.

Maggie slowed and turned onto what couldn't even be considered a road. Wind and rain had eroded the tire tracks into jagged crevices in the prairie landscape. Concentrating on straddling the worse of the ruts, Maggie maneuvered through the twists and turns. The hills were steeper here and she couldn't see anything but the track in front of her and the rolling slopes of frosted prairie grass. As the trail led over the top of a hill, a rugged rock bluff appeared ahead, rising above the prairie in majestic glory, tinged red and orange with the rays of the setting sun.

At the base of the cliff was a dilapidated shack with a stream of smoke curling from a narrow chimney.

Maggie swallowed hard. Her child had been weathering the early-winter freezing temperatures in a shack heated by nothing more than a wood-burning fireplace? She wanted to reach over and smack Leotie for exposing her son to the danger of fire and sickness. But she kept her hands on the wheel, her foot getting heavier on the accelerator as the road flattened and they moved closer to the shack where she'd find her son.

A shiny white Lexus SUV stood in front of the building. "I take it that isn't your mother's car."

Leotie only shrugged, refusing to respond.

So this was a setup and Leotie was in on this kidnapping with someone else. Given that the caller had been male, Maggie had guessed this. Again, she wished she'd gone straight to the station and Joe. Was it too late for her to turn around and go back for help?

A light flickered in the window as someone peered through the cloth covering. Too late to turn around and get help. Whoever was in that shack had seen her vehicle and knew she was out here. If he got nervous, he might decide the baby was too much of a liability.

Maggie refused to think of what Leotie's accomplice would do to Dakota. She couldn't turn back, she had to know her baby was all right, even if it meant walking into a trap.

How could she go into that building on an equal footing with whoever was holding her son? She could hold a knife to Leotie's throat and walk in there demanding a trade, if she had a knife.

Both Leotie and her accomplice had to know they had her over a barrel. She wouldn't do anything to jeopardize her son's life. She touched a hand to her pocket where the memory stick rested, her only bargaining chip.

All she could do was walk in and hope she could get to her son and maybe talk these people out of hurting him. Maybe she could trade her life for his. Surely even monsters didn't kill helpless babies.

Maggie shifted her car into Park and sat for a moment, her mind sifting through all the possibilities without a single solution surfacing.

"This is it, isn't it? Even if you get your son back, you won't get Joe. He'll never forgive you for lying to him about his child."

At this particular point, Maggie could only concentrate on her son. She loved Joe and she wanted him to be a part of his son's life. But one hurdle at a time. Get Dakota to safety and then try to straighten out the mess her life had become.

"He'll hate you forever," Leotie said, her voice digging into Maggie's nerves.

"That's a chance I'll have to take." She opened her door. "Come on. You're going in first."

Leotie climbed out of the little car and led the way at a slow saunter to the tiny building. She lifted her hand and knocked once. "It's me, Leotie. Let me in."

The door swung open, light from an oil lantern spilling out into the dusk.

Maggie craned her neck to peer over Leotie's shoulder, desperate to see her son.

Leotie stepped inside, leaving Maggie on the threshold. A large hand snaked out and grabbed her arm, yanking her inside, where she faced Gray Running Fox.

"You!"

Gray's tailored suit seemed out of place next to the rough-hewn boards and the sparse wooden furniture in the dilapidated building. His eyes were wide and bloodshot and his mouth twisted into a sneer. "Yeah, me."

Her surprise turned to anger. The manager of the Grand

Buffalo Casino had threatened her son all for a tiny storage device she could pick up at a store for under a hundred dollars. "Where is he? Where's my baby?"

"Do you have what your husband stole?" He tugged at the tie around his neck, loosening the knot until it hung at an angle. His movements were erratic and disjointed, as if he was nervous or not feeling well.

Maggie's eyes narrowed, "Tell me what it is, and I'll tell you whether I have it."

He got in her face and hissed, "He stole information he had no right to. I want it back."

Swallowing her fear, she demanded, "Show me my baby."

He jerked his head toward Leotie. "Get the kid."

Leotie's lips thinned and she opened her mouth to say something but Gray cut her off.

"Get the damned kid!"

Red splotches appeared high on her cheekbones and she looked as if she wanted to argue. Instead she walked to the back of the little shack and disappeared behind a curtain hung over the door separating the living area from the sleeping area. Would Leotie bring out the baby? The woman was mean and spiteful to adults, but would she hurt a child?

Maggie took a step in her direction, only to be stopped by a hand on her arm. "I want that database."

"Obviously enough to kill innocent people!" Maggie tried to shake her arm to free it from his claw-like grip.

Gray held on, refusing to let go. "Give me the database!"

"Why, so you can kill me and my son anyway?" She forced herself to sound tough when inside she was shaking like a leaf in a forty-mile-an-hour wind. "Did you think I was stupid enough to bring it with me?"

"On the contrary, I think you were smart enough to know we'd kill your baby if you didn't." His fingers dug into her flesh. "Where is the database?"

"On its way to the state crime lab, Gray." She stared up at him, her gaze cold and angry. "The game's over. You've been caught."

Gray dropped her arm and stepped back, pushing a shaky hand through his dark hair. "You're lying." Beneath his swarthy skin, the Native American man looked green. Had she struck a nerve? Could she strike again without retaliation?

"Why would I lie to you?" She advanced toward him. "I knew if you got hold of the database you'd have no further use of me and wouldn't want witnesses." *Please let my bluff work.* If he caught on, she'd be in deep trouble.

"Don't listen to her. She's pulling your chain and you're just gullible enough to fall for it." Leotie stood in the doorway with a bundle in her arms.

Maggie's heart rose in her throat, threatening to cut off her air. She recognized the blanket Winona had made for Dakota and the tiny nose and cheeks peeking out as those of her son. "Dakota!" She reached out for her child, her arms aching to hold him.

"Not so fast." Leotie turned away, blocking Maggie's attempt to claim her son. "He's our insurance policy to get us out of here alive."

"If she's already turned in the information storage device, we're dead," Gray said, collapsing onto a bench in front of a table made from stumps and rough-hewn planks. He buried his face in his hands, his shoulders shaking. "Marcus will kill us."

"Speak for yourself. I don't plan on dying here. If it comes down to it, I'll use this baby as my ticket out."

"How?" Gray looked up, his face drawn and looking much older than his mid-thirties. "Caldwell's men are everywhere. They'll find us and kill us."

"They'll find you. And you should have thought of that before you sold out to him," Leotie said.

"I didn't have a choice," he said, shoving a hand through his dark hair. "It was go along with him or go to prison."

"Just like Murray." Leotie snorted. "You fail to remember that you wouldn't be under Marcus's 'protection' if you hadn't gotten so caught up in the drugs."

"Shut up, Leotie." He pushed to his feet, his body swaying unsteadily. "Shut up!"

"And were you strung out on drugs when you slipped and let Paul into the database? You were, weren't you? You screwed it up, didn't you?" Leotie shook her head. "All for a high. You had to have your freakin' high."

Dakota stirred and let out a small cry.

Maggie reached out for her child. "Let me have my son. He doesn't have anything to do with this. He's just a baby."

Hearing his mother's voice, Dakota's cries intensified until his screams filled the little house.

"Can you shut him up?" Gray slapped his hands over his ears. "Just shut him up!"

Leotie turned to the room behind her. "Take the kid and pack his things, we're getting out of here."

A small, gray-haired Lakota woman stepped up behind Leotie and took the child from her. "What you're doing is wrong, Leotie. Let this woman have her child."

"Shut up! I don't need you telling me what to do. I've

had that long enough with him." She jerked her head toward Gray. "And I'm done taking orders."

"You can talk big, Leotie, but when it comes down to it, you're going to jail for murder," Gray said. "I didn't sign on this gig to kill anyone."

"Oh, get a grip, Gray," Leotie said, her face twisted into a smirk. "Shoot up some more of those drugs you can't live without so maybe when you die, you won't feel a thing."

"I didn't kill anyone. That was all your doing." Gray pointed a shaking finger at the young Lakota woman. "You're the one who ran Paul off the road and you're the one who shot the others. I might have stolen money and taken drugs, but you're the one who'll do life for murder."

Leotie laughed. "I'm not doing life because I'm not going to jail."

"You killed Paul?" Maggie asked, her voice shaking with the force of emotion welling up inside her.

"That do-gooder stuck his nose in where it didn't belong," Leotie spat out. "He was going to turn us all in."

"That would have been the end of it if you had gotten the database from him first," Gray said.

"I didn't see *you* coming up with any ideas," Leotie said.

"You didn't give me a chance," Gray said. "You had to jump the gun and do it yourself. If you'd left it to me, I could have gotten the database back without killing anyone."

Leotie snorted. "You couldn't find your way out of the meth long enough to figure out your employee was going to rat on you."

Maggie watched the two volleying jibes at each other like a couple of players in a tennis match. If they stayed distracted long enough, she might figure out a way to get Dakota out of there.

"I would have stayed clean if not for you," Gray said.

Leotie's eyes rolled upward. "You're a junkie, Gray. If I hadn't supplied, you'd have found another way."

"Not when you're the only supplier on the reservation, Tokala."

Maggie's head spun with the overload of information. So Leotie had been the dealer all along. She'd assumed Tokala was male.

"Don't look so shocked, little miss social worker." Leotie flicked her hair over her shoulder. "I've been dealing since I was fifteen."

"You were just a girl," Maggie said, her heart aching for the young Leotie, despite what she'd done to her and her son.

"I should kill you now for bringing a bag full of talcum powder instead of my stash of meth. Do you know how much that cost me to make?"

"I don't care what it cost. I hope the cops flushed it down the toilet. You're killing kids with that stuff." Blood flushed over Maggie's eyes as anger burned a path through her system. "Did you kill Bill Franks to get it?"

"I wouldn't have had to if that damned brat, Charlie, hadn't stolen my stash. And I sure as hell wasn't giving Franks a cut."

"Wow," Maggie shook her head, staring at the woman as if seeing her for the first time. "You really are a monster."

"I guess you'd think so, with your holier-than-thou attitude. I call it taking care of myself."

"I call it sick," Maggie said.

"Frankly, I don't care what you call it. I'll be taking the baby as insurance that I get away."

The thought of Leotie having control of her baby froze Maggie's blood in her veins. "Please let my baby go. You can take me as leverage, just leave Dakota. He's innocent."

"No one's innocent," Leotie said. "Besides, he'll need me because he won't have a mother or a father around after today. Joe should have been mine, but no, he wanted you instead. Taking his son to raise as my own will be the best revenge. Wouldn't that just kill him to know?" Her brows rose. "But then he'll be dead anyway. Just like Paul, Bernie, Franks and you." Leotie raised the gun to point at Maggie's chest.

With no time to think, Maggie flung herself to the side.

The deafening sound of the gun going off blasted her ears at the same time as the bullet nicked her rib. Maggie fell to the floor, her head hitting hard enough she saw stars, and then darkness closed in around her. *No, you can't pass out. Dakota needs you.*

Chapter Eighteen

Joe parked on the other side of the hill from the bluff and hiked in to the hunting cabin. Maggie's car stood with the doors wide open and the interior light spreading a meager slant of light onto the ground. Gray's Lexus stood next to it. Darkness covered the land in a shroud providing good concealment all the way to the corner of the house. With backup still ten minutes away, Joe couldn't risk waiting.

As he crept toward the building, Joe heard people talking inside. The angry voices of Leotie and Gray carried through the walls. Peering through a small gap in the only window still intact and not boarded up, he could see Leotie holding a baby in a baby blanket. Then she handed the child to another person Joe couldn't see.

The shiny glint of metal flashed in the muted lighting, slicing straight into Joe's heart. Leotie pointed a gun at someone outside Joe's line of sight. Despite the sub-zero temperatures, sweat broke out on Joe's brow and fear consumed him: fear for Maggie and fear for the son he hadn't known about until today.

Adrenaline surged through his body, and before he

could think through a plan, he leaped up from his position by the window and charged for the door.

As he reached for the handle, a shot rang out.

No!

Joe rammed his shoulder into the door. The rusty catch gave way beneath his weight and the door flung wide.

Leotie screamed and aimed the weapon at Joe. She took a deep breath and her hand steadied. "About time you showed up to rescue your girlfriend. But I'm afraid you're a little late."

Joe's gaze fell to Maggie lying on the floor in the little room, a dark stain spreading out from the hole in her powder-blue winter jacket. When Joe lurched toward her, Leotie cleared her throat.

"I wouldn't do that," she said.

Joe stared at Maggie, longing to go to her. "She's hurt."

"No, she's dead. Just like you will be." Raising the barrel to aim at Joe's heart, she braced her right hand in the palm of her left. "For too long, I wanted you. You didn't even see me."

Anger welled up inside him. "I saw you, Leotie. I just didn't like what I saw."

"I loved you!" she screamed.

Joe snorted. "You don't know the meaning of love." A baby cried in the room behind a curtain. Was it Dakota? His son?

"And you do?" Leotie laughed. "You've walked away from every woman you ever dated. How can you know about love?"

"I learned by watching someone who really cares." Maggie, whose eyes flickered. Was she alive?

"Maggie?" Leotie's laugh sounded harsh in the quiet interior of the old cabin. "You swore on your father's deathbed you'd never marry an outsider. She's not Lakota."

"Unlike you, I learn from my mistakes. I learned that it doesn't matter. Love is a gift not to be taken lightly."

"And you blew it." Leotie's laugh rose to an unnatural pitch, bordering on hysterical. "It's ironic isn't it? I couldn't have you. Now you can't have her." Leotie's hands moved with her words and the gun shifted its aim from Joe's chest.

Out of the corner of his eye, Joe could see Maggie's body tense. He had to keep Leotie's attention so she wouldn't try to finish off the woman on the floor.

"That's the way you've always been, Leotie, and the reason I could never love you. It's all about you. And if you don't get your way, you hurt others. Just like you killed Paul."

"He was going to blow open our little operation. He had to go," Leotie said.

"And what happened that made you go after Tom and Bernie?"

"Are you doing your cop thing and interrogating me?" Her brows rose and she smiled. "'Cause I'm not talking."

Gray stepped forward. "She was there when Tom and Bernie saw me pass money to Marcus Caldwell. She also killed Kiya."

With an unobtrusive wave, Joe motioned Maggie to remain inert. "Why?" he asked.

"Because Kiya found out she was the one supplying drugs to the kids, isn't that right, Leotie? She was the one keeping me in meth as well."

"Shut up, Gray! You talk too much."

"You're the one that did all the killing. I didn't. I'm not going down with you for murder."

While Leotie's attention was directed to Gray, Maggie's leg scooted closer to Leotie until it was only a foot away.

Joe inched closer as well.

"Leotie, this has gone far enough," Gray walked toward her. "I won't let you kill another person. Give me that gun."

"You don't have a choice anymore, Gray. You and I could have been a team, but you couldn't stay clean. And drugs make you sloppy. Sloppy, like letting Paul steal the data and Tom and Bernie see you paying Marcus."

"Give it up, Leotie," Gray said softly. He reached out to take the gun from Leotie. "There is too much evidence against us and I'm sure Joe has more cops on their way." His hands wrapped around hers and he stared into her eyes. "It's over."

Leotie's body stiffened. "Maybe for you." She squeezed the trigger.

The force of the bullet sent Gray staggering backward, clutching at his chest, his eyes wide and glazed. His legs buckled and he collapsed against the worn plank flooring.

Before Leotie could turn toward Joe, Maggie kicked out, her foot aiming for Leotie's kneecaps and connecting hard enough to send the woman toppling over. At the same time, Joe lunged for Leotie and the gun.

Gunfire echoed off the walls, the sound ringing in Joe's eardrums.

Leotie screamed, dropping to the floor. But she still held tightly to the weapon, tears streaming down her face. "I should have killed her. It's all her fault."

Joe wrested the gun from her hands, dropped the clip

and emptied the barrel before tucking it into the back of his belt. Then he went to Maggie's side.

Leotie struggled to rise and her face contorted as she fell back. "What did you do to my knee?" Her back arched and she wailed, "I should have killed you."

"But you didn't," Maggie said, a smile spreading across her face.

Joe inhaled for the first time in what seemed like hours. "Are you all right?" He pushed her jacket aside and looked down at the blood soaked into her shirt. The baby crying in the back room was an assuring sound.

"It looks worse than it is," she said. "It just nicked my side. It can wait. I want to see my son."

"You're no good to your son if you pass out while holding him. Let me see." He eased the ruined sweater upward until he could see where her skin was torn and bleeding. His heart stuttered as he realized how close he had been to losing her. He stripped off his jacket, uniform shirt and finally his white T-shirt, leaving his chest bare.

"See? It's not so bad." She smiled and looked up at him. Then her smile faded, a sad look dulling the shine in her eyes. "Joe, I'm sorry I didn't tell you about Dakota. He's your son, not Paul's, and you had every right to know."

Joe wadded his T-shirt and pressed it against her wound. Several long seconds stretched by with all the emotions of the past four days threatening to choke his vocal chords.

"Don't listen to her, Joe," Leotie called out from her position on the floor. "She's lied to you before, she'll lie to you again."

After shooting a piercing glare at the other woman, Joe

turned his gaze back to Maggie. "Let's get Dakota and get you two home. Then we'll talk."

Maggie's hand reached out and curved around his arm. "Fair enough."

He hurried over to Gray who lay at an odd angle on the rough planks of the wooden floor with a gunshot wound to his chest. Joe pressed a hand to his carotid artery and couldn't find a pulse. Gray Running Fox was dead.

"What about me?" Leotie whined. "I can't move."

Joe ignored her and moved back to Maggie.

The curtain over the door to the back room opened and Leotie's mother peered out, her dark eyes wide, her hands trembling. "Is it safe to come out? Have you stopped shoot—" When she saw Leotie lying on the floor, she cried out and dropped down beside her.

The baby wailed.

Maggie's grip tightened on Joe's arm. "Help me up."

He pressed her down. "You shouldn't move until we get an ambulance out here." He pressed the button on his radio. "Del? How far are you from the cabin?"

Del's voice sounded over the radio. "I can see it now. Everything okay?"

"It is now." He stared over at Maggie, hoping he was right. If all went well, he'd have her home by tomorrow. That's when the hard stuff would come. Their talk. "Call for ambulances. We have three people down."

The wailing intensified from the other room and Maggie brushed his hands aside and struggled to her feet.

"You're bleeding and standing isn't helping that wound." Joe's arm curved around her waist and he leaned her against him.

"I don't care. I want my baby." Wincing with each step, she worked her way toward the room where Dakota was sending up a howling siren of a call.

In all the chaos of the gunfire, Joe had almost forgotten about the baby. Now as he stared down at the small baby lying on the bunk, he knew fear greater than any gun pointed at his chest. This was his child. His son. He was responsible for protecting him, providing for him and teaching him everything he needed to know to live in the world and on this reservation as a member of the Lakota tribe. If Maggie would let him.

When Maggie reached out to take the baby, Joe held her back. She looked up at him, a question in her eyes.

"May I hold my son?" he asked.

Her eyes glistened as she nodded and stepped back.

As if he might break him, Joe lifted the squirming bundle that barely filled his hands and held him up to the light of the candle on the table beside the bed. "He has his mother's hair."

"He has his father's skin and eyes."

Joe nodded. Dark-brown eyes stared back at him from a light, creamy-mocha face.

Dakota cooed, blowing a bubble from his rosy lips.

His heart near bursting, Joe turned to Maggie. "He's beautiful."

Tears slid down Maggie's face as she reached out for her baby. "I know."

The front door opened and more people filled the outer room. Del stepped into the door frame and smiled at Joe. "I see you've finally figured it out."

"You knew?" Joe asked. The joy of discovering his son

smoothed the edge off whatever anger he might have felt toward Del for not telling him sooner.

"Hell, everyone on the reservation knew." Del shook his head. "You were too blind to see it and too dense to do the numbers."

"Is this true?" Joe asked Maggie.

Maggie's lips twisted into a wry grin as she looked up from examining her son. "I had no idea they'd guessed until Dakota disappeared."

Del thwacked him on the back, grinning. "Congratulations, boss."

MAGGIE STAYED OVERNIGHT in the reservation hospital with Dakota in the same room. She didn't want him out of her sight for a moment. Even though Leotie had just been transferred to a hospital in Rapid City, Maggie knew it would be a long time before she'd be able to leave her baby in another room, out of reach.

She'd spent half the night staring down at him in his bed, where he slept as though nothing major had happened over the past few days. The other half of the night she'd tried to sleep, only to jump up every time he so much as whimpered. By morning, all she wanted was to go home.

Her rib was bruised and she had to have two stitches to close the wound, but she was more than ready to get on with her life and return to a mundane routine. She'd had enough excitement to last for a long time.

What worried her most was that Joe hadn't been by to see her after he'd ridden to the hospital in the back of the ambulance with her and Dakota. Once she got to the hospital she'd given him the memory stick and the key to the safe deposit box for the backup. As soon as he knew she was settled and in capable hands, he'd left. He hadn't been back that night and it was well past noon.

Was he still angry she'd kept his son from him? She wouldn't blame him. She wished he'd at least come by so she could tell him her reasons, not that they'd make any difference.

Now that she had her son back, she had to face the possibility his father would want custody. Tears welled in Maggie's eyes and one dropped down on the soft blue baby blanket covering her son. How could she keep her child from his father?

She knew Joe would make a wonderful father and she had no doubt he'd love, protect and provide for Dakota. But would he want his son's mother in his life as well? Could he forgive her?

Could he love her even though she wasn't Lakota?

A knock on the door to her hospital room set her heart fluttering in her chest. Was it Joe?

Winona Little Elk poked her head around the door. "Up for a visitor?"

Maggie took a shaky breath to calm herself. "Yes, come in."

Winona carried a plastic grocery bag filled with clean clothes. "Temperature's around thirteen degrees and it's snowing. I thought you'd like to wear something besides that hospital gown when you leave here."

"Thank you, Winona." Maggie dug through the clothes, finding jeans, a sweater and fresh underwear. At the bottom, she found fresh clothes for Dakota as well. Her eyes filled with tears as she recognized the powder-blue fleece shirt and pants she'd purchased in Rapid City before Paul's death. Buying clothes for Dakota was fun and she loved talking to him as they strolled around the mall.

She wondered what it would be like if Joe went with her. A family outing. "Could you watch Dakota?"

Winona lifted the little blue shirt. "Of course. Go on, we'll be just fine. Won't we, *hoksika?*" She tickled Dakota's chin and he smiled up at her.

Gulping back a sob, Maggie grabbed her clothes and retreated to the bathroom to change, careful not to disturb her stitches or allow any more tears to fall. Hadn't she cried enough in the last few days for a lifetime? No matter what happened with Joe, she'd survive. Her son would be her focus.

Joe would want joint custody.

Maggie had thought all she wanted was her son back in her life, and everything else would work out. But there was so much still up in the air, she felt like a complete mess on the inside.

At the crux of it all was the fact she still loved Joe. Shoot, she'd never stopped loving him. That's why she'd stayed married in name only to Paul, refusing to let him past the wall of her indifference to him.

And where *was* Joe? He'd promised they'd talk, but he hadn't even made the effort to come by and see her.

Running her fingers through her tangled hair, Maggie paused to stare at herself in the mirror. She was a wreck, and the tears she tried to stop kept welling up in her eyes. After a quick dab at the moisture in her eyes with a tissue, she exited the bathroom.

"Good, you look much more like yourself." Winona

held Dakota up for her inspection, his smile bringing out a smile from Maggie in spite of her confused feelings. How could she be unhappy when her baby was back?

Winona handed Dakota to her and gathered all her belongings. "My orders were to take you home."

"Orders?" Maggie laid her son on the bed and eased his hands and feet into the bunting coat Winona had brought as well, tucking him safely beneath the fleece. "I've never known you to take orders from anyone." She zipped the bunting up the front and adjusted the hood over her son's head.

"The chief of the tribal police ordered me to take you home while he finishes cleaning up after Leotie, Gray and Murray."

"Oh." Maggie straightened, settling Dakota into her arms. So, Joe was thinking about her. He hadn't forgotten. "I guess he's pretty busy?"

"A mountain of paperwork and he had to work with the state police and FBI to bring Marcus Caldwell in as well."

The entire time Maggie had been worrying why Joe hadn't been by to see her, he'd been doing his job and wrapping up the details.

Her thoughts were a little brighter as she pulled on her damaged jacket. One of the nurses had wiped as much of the blood away as she could, but it would have to be replaced. The hole in the side would always be there to remind her how close she'd come to losing both Dakota and Joe.

Fastening the zipper up the front, she turned and smiled at Winona. "I'm ready."

JOE STARED at the mound of paperwork sitting on his desk and ran a hand over his face, feeling every one of his thirty-one years and a few more. Sleep was something to look forward to after everything was nailed down, and the perpetrators were either in the morgue, the hospital or locked away.

Marcus Caldwell had been sleeping peacefully in his home in Rapid City when the state police and the FBI had arrived to read him his rights.

The representative of the National Indian Gaming Commission denied all involvement, but with Tom's eyewitness testimony of the money exchange and Leotie's confession, they had enough evidence to bring him to trial. Agent Metcalf had done more digging into the Lucky You Casino, finding that a certain Marcus Caldwell was a part owner, and he had been the one to drop the embezzlement charges against Murray. He had also been the one who'd transferred Assistant Casino Manager Gray Running Fox to the Grand Buffalo Casino on the Painted Rock Reservation after he'd been suspended from his job for failing his drug test.

Halfway through the reports, Joe realized he was putting off the inevitable—his talk with Maggie.

He knew how he felt, knew he wanted her in his life forever. What scared the starch out of him was he didn't have a clue how she felt about him.

Del strode into the office, just in from his trip to Rapid City following the ambulance carrying Leotie Jones. "What are you still doing here?"

"Paperwork," Joe muttered, not really interested in idle conversation, preferring to wallow in the limbo of his relationship with Maggie all by himself.

"I'd have thought you'd be with Maggie."

"Well, I'm not." He tapped his pen on the form in front

of him, making enough noise that Del could figure out his interference wasn't wanted.

"What's wrong with you, man?" Del pulled up a chair next to Joe's and straddled it. "You love her, don't you?"

Joe shot him a quelling look. "I don't want to talk about it."

"Do you or don't you?"

"Of course I do, not that it's any of your business." His mood grew more sullen with Del sitting next to him like a pesky thorn in his side.

"Then why aren't you over at her place begging her to take you back?"

"Easy for you to say. You weren't the one who told her over a year ago that she didn't have a place in your life."

"So you tell her you were wrong and ask her to forgive you."

Joe slammed his pen to the desk and stood so fast his seat fell over backward. "I did, and she didn't."

Del stood, too, relentless in his attack. "Before or after you knew about the baby?"

"Before." Where was the officer going with this?

Del sat back in his chair. "Well, there you go."

"There I go where?" Joe scrubbed a hand through his hair.

"She didn't forgive you then because she had the secret of your son eating at her. She couldn't forgive you when she probably thought you wouldn't forgive her."

Del's words were making too much sense. Problem was Joe didn't want to listen to someone making sense. He wanted to wallow a little longer in his confusion. "What if she doesn't want me in her life?"

"What if I do?" a soft voice said behind him.

Joe spun around so fast he nearly tripped on the over-turned chair. "Maggie?"

"Yeah, Joe. And here I was thinking you weren't interested in me or your son."

He stood motionless in the middle of the cluttered office, a myriad of emotions coursing through his brain. How could she think he wasn't interested in her or his son? "Are you out of your mind?"

"Yeah," she said, a tentative smile lighting her face. "Out of my mind crazy in love with one Lakota Indian who melts my heart."

"Uh, do you two want to be alone?" Del asked, pushing to his feet, his cheeks flushed red beneath the dark coloring of his heritage.

"No, stay," Joe ordered.

"Why make him stay? Are you afraid I'll tell you to get lost, and that I don't want to be a part of your life?" Maggie asked.

"As a matter of fact—"

Del elbowed him in the ribs. "Don't screw this up, too, boss."

"What I meant was…" His gaze darted to all four corners of the room before it came back to rest on the woman he'd come to love more than life itself. He set the chair on its legs and strode toward Maggie and his son. "What I meant to say is…ah, hell. Maggie, I love you."

"Even if Dakota wasn't your son?" she asked, staring up into his eyes, as if sending him a silent plea.

"Yes."

"There." Del clapped Joe on the back. "Now you have it out in the open. That wasn't so hard, was it?"

"You can leave now, Del." Joe said without taking his gaze off Maggie and Dakota.

"I thought you wanted me to stay," Del said, a grin spilling across his face.

"Beat it, Del," Maggie said, closing the gap between her and Joe. "Unless you want to stick around for some really noisy kissing."

Before Del could come up with a glib response, Joe sent a withering glance his way.

"Okay, okay. I'm leaving." Del shrugged into his coat and gloves. "Sheesh, why don't you two get a room?"

With his gaze back on Maggie, Joe answered, "We will, once we get a few things straight."

"Let me know how straight you get 'em. I'll be out chasing buffalo on the prairie."

"Good." Joe pulled Maggie and Dakota into his arms as the door closed behind Del. "Finally, we're alone."

Dakota stared up at Joe, his eyes wide and inquisitive. Joe's own eyes filled to overflowing with the love he felt for this woman and their child. "I love you, Maggie. If I hadn't been such a fool before I left for Iraq, I'd have realized it then. Can you forgive me?"

"Only if you can forgive me for not telling you about your son." She stared down at a button on his chest. "When you said you didn't want me as part of your life, I was heartbroken. Two days after you left, I realized I was pregnant. I didn't know what to do. I'd already lost you, I couldn't stand the thought of losing your child, too."

When Joe started to speak, Maggie pressed a hand to his lips. "Let me finish."

He kissed her fingers and remained silent.

"I was afraid if you knew, you'd sue for custody and take my child away from me. Then I would have lost you and my baby. I couldn't stand that. I was afraid."

"Yet you stayed on the reservation? Why?"

She shrugged. "The kids needed me. I had been working so closely with Kiya to get her off drugs and into school. If I'd left then, all her hard work would have been for nothing." A tear rolled down her cheek.

"Leotie killed Kiya. She didn't overdose on drugs by herself."

"I know." Maggie shifted Dakota in her arms. "I thought the only way I could stay and avoid anyone finding out about Dakota was to marry a white man."

"Paul."

"After you left, he started hanging around. I think he truly loved me, Joe." More tears slid down her cheeks.

Joe wanted to kiss her and take away her pain.

"Paul was good to me. He never asked for anything I wasn't willing to give. I just wish I could have loved him the way he deserved."

"Me, too," Joe said. He should have been a better brother to the man when he was alive.

She continued as if she hadn't heard his comment. "I couldn't love Paul because I never stopped loving you. He deserved to be loved and I failed him. Now he's dead."

"But we aren't and we have a son who needs us." Joe lifted Dakota in one arm and with the other, pulled Maggie close. "Do you think you could be happy living on a reservation?"

"If I'm with you, and if you promise to teach our son the ways of his ancestors."

"Conditions, huh?" He smiled. "I can live with that."

Leaning close, he pressed a quick kiss on her lips before he straightened and stared into her eyes. "I love you, Maggie. Will you marry me?"

"I thought you'd never ask."

* * * * *

*Experience entertaining women's fiction
for every woman who has wondered
"what's next?" in their lives.
Turn the page for a sneak preview of
a new book from Harlequin NEXT,
WHY IS MURDER ON THE MENU, ANYWAY?
by Stevi Mittman*

On sale December 26, wherever books are sold.

"Now that's the kind of man you should be looking for,"
my mother, the self-appointed keeper of my shelf-life
stamp, says. She points with her fork at a man in the corner
of the Steak-Out Restaurant, a dive I've just been hired to
redecorate. Making this restaurant look four-star will be
hard, but not half as hard as getting through lunch without
strangling the woman across the table from me. "*He* would
make a good husband."

"Oh, you can tell that from across the room?" I ask,
wondering how it is she can forget that when we had
trouble getting rid of my last husband, she shot him.
"Besides being ten minutes away from death if he actually
eats all that steak, he's twenty years too old for me and—

shallow woman that I am—twenty pounds too heavy. Besides, I am *so* not looking for another husband here. I'm looking to design a new image for this place, looking for some sense of ambience, some feeling, something I can build a proposal on for them."

My mother studies the man in the corner, tilting her head, the better to gauge his age, I suppose. I think she's grimacing, but with all the Botox and Restylane injected into that face, it's hard to tell. She takes another bite of her steak salad, chews slowly so that I don't miss the fact that the steak is a poor cut and tougher than it should be. "You're concentrating on the wrong kind of proposal," she says finally. "Just look at this place, Teddi. It's a dive. There are hardly any other diners. What does *that* tell you about the food?"

"That they cater to a dinner crowd and it's lunchtime," I tell her.

I don't know what I was thinking bringing her here with me. I suppose I thought it would be better than eating alone. There really are days when my common sense goes on vacation. Clearly, this is one of them. I mean, really, did I not resolve less than three weeks ago that I would not let my mother get to me anymore?

What good are New Year's resolutions, anyway?

Mario approaches the man's table and my mother studies him while they converse. Eventually Mario leaves the table with a huff, after which the diner glances up and meets my mother's gaze. I think she's smiling at him. That or she's got indigestion. They size each other up.

I concentrate on making sketches in my notebook and try to ignore the fact that my mother is flirting. At nearly seventy, she's developed an unhealthy interest in members of the opposite sex to whom she isn't married.

According to my father, who has broken the TMI rule and given me Too Much Information, she has no interest in sex with him. Better, I suppose, to be clued in on what they aren't doing in the bedroom than have to hear what they might be doing.

"He's not so old," my mother says, noticing that I have barely touched the Chinese chicken salad she warned me not to get. "He's got about as many years on you as you have on your little cop friend."

She does this to make me crazy. I know it, but it works all the same. "Drew Scoones is not my little 'friend.' He's a detective with whom I—"

"Screwed around," my mother says. I must look shocked, because my mother laughs at me and asks if I think she doesn't know the "lingo."

What I thought she didn't know was that Drew and I actually tangled in the sheets. And, since it's possible she's just fishing, I sidestep the issue and tell her that Drew is just a couple of years younger than me and that I don't need reminding. I dig into my salad with renewed vigor, determined to show my mother that Chinese chicken salad in a steak place was not the stupid choice it's proving to be.

After a few more minutes of my picking at the wilted leaves on my plate, the man my mother has me nearly engaged to pays his bill and heads past us toward the back of the restaurant. I watch my mother take in his shoes, his suit and the diamond pinkie ring that seems to be cutting off the circulation in his little finger.

"Such nice hands," she says after the man is out of sight.

"Manicured." She and I both stare at my hands. I have two popped acrylics that are being held on at weird angles by bandages. My cuticles are ragged and there's marker decorating my right hand from measuring carelessly when I did a drawing for a customer.

Twenty minutes later she's disappointed that he managed to leave the restaurant without our noticing. He will join the list of the ones I let get away. I will hear about him twenty years from now when—according to my mother—my children will be grown and I will still be single, living pathetically alone with several dogs and cats.

After my ex, that sounds good to me.

The waitress tells us that our meal has been taken care of by the management and, after thanking Mario, the owner, complimenting him on the wonderful meal and assuring him that once I have redecorated his place people will be flocking here in droves (I actually use those words and ignore my mother when she rolls her eyes), my mother and I head for the restroom.

My father—unfortunately not with us today—has the patience of a saint. He got it over the years of living with my mother. She, perhaps as a result, figures he has the patience for both of them, and feels justified having none. For her, no rules apply, and a little thing like a picture of a man on the door to a public restroom is certainly no barrier to using the john. In all fairness, it does seem silly to stand and wait for the ladies' room if no one is using the men's room.

Still, it's the idea that rules don't apply to her, signs don't apply to her, conventions don't apply to her. She knocks on the door to the men's room. When no one answers she gestures to me to go in ahead. I tell her that I can certainly wait for the ladies' room to be free and she shrugs and goes in herself.

Not a minute later there is a bloodcurdling scream from behind the men's room door.

"Mom!" I yell. "Are you all right?"

Mario comes running over, the waitress on his heels. Two customers head our way while my mother continues to scream.

I try the door, but it is locked. I yell for her to open it and she fumbles with the knob. When she finally manages to unlock and open it, she is white behind her two streaks of blush, but she is on her feet and appears shaken but not stirred.

"What happened?" I ask her. So do Mario and the waitress and the few customers who have migrated to the back of the place.

She points toward the bathroom and I go in, thinking it serves her right for using the men's room. But I see nothing amiss.

She gestures toward the stall, and, like any self-respecting and suspicious woman, I poke the door open with one finger, expecting the worst.

What I find is worse than the worst.

The husband my mother picked out for me is sitting on the toilet. His pants are puddled around his ankles, his hands are hanging at his sides. Pinned to his chest is some sort of Health Department certificate.

Oh, and there is a large, round, bloodless bullet hole between his eyes.

* * *

Four Nassau County police officers are securing the area, waiting for the detectives and crime scene personnel to show up. They are trying, though not very hard, to comfort my mother, who in another era would be considered to be suffering from the vapors. Less tactful in the twenty-first century, I'd say she was losing it. That is, if I didn't know her better, know she was milking it for everything it was worth.

My mother loves attention. As it begins to flag, she swoons and claims to feel faint. Despite four No Smoking signs, my mother insists it's all right for her to light up because, after all, she's in shock. Not to mention that signs, as we know, don't apply to her.

When asked not to smoke, she collapses mournfully in a chair and lets her head loll to the side, all without mussing her hair.

Eventually, the detectives show up to find the four patrolmen all circled around her, debating whether to administer CPR, smelling salts or simply call the paramedics. I, however, know just what will snap her to attention.

"Detective Scoones," I say loudly. My mother parts the sea of cops.

"We have to stop meeting like this," he says lightly to me, but I can feel him checking me over with his eyes, making sure I'm all right while pretending not to care.

"What have you got in those pants?" my mother asks him, coming to her feet and staring at his crotch accusingly. "*Baydar?* Everywhere we Bayers are, you turn up. You don't expect me to buy that this is a coincidence, I hope."

Drew tells my mother that it's nice to see her, too, and asks if it's his fault that her daughter seems to attract disasters.

Charming to be made to feel like the bearer of a plague. He asks how I am.

"Just peachy," I tell him. "I seem to be making a habit of finding dead bodies, my mother is driving me crazy and the catering hall I booked two freakin' years ago for Dana's bat mitzvah has just been shut down by the Board of Health!"

"Glad to see your luck's finally changing," he says, giving me a quick squeeze around the shoulders before turning his attention to the patrolmen, asking what they've got, whether they've taken any statements, moved anything, all the sort of stuff you see on TV, without any of the drama. That is, if you don't count my mother's threats to faint every few minutes when she senses no one's paying attention to her.

Mario tells his waitsstaff to bring everyone espresso, which I decline because I'm wired enough. Drew pulls him aside and a minute later I'm handed a cup of coffee that smells divinely of Kahlúa.

The man knows me well. Too well.

His partner, whom I've met once or twice, says he'll interview the kitchen staff. Drew asks Mario if he minds if he takes statements from the patrons first and gets to him and the waitstaff afterward.

"No, no," Mario tells him. "Do the patrons first." Drew raises his eyebrow at me like he wants to know if I get the double entendre. I try to look bored.

"What is it with you and murder victims?" he asks me when we sit down at a table in the corner.

I search them out so that I can see you again, I almost say, but I'm afraid it will sound desperate instead of sarcastic.

My mother, lighting up and daring him with a look to tell her not to, reminds him that *she* was the one to find the body.

Drew asks what happened *this time*. My mother tells him how the man in the john was "taken" with me, couldn't take his eyes off me and blatantly flirted with both of us. To his credit, Drew doesn't laugh, but his smirk is undeniable to the trained eye. And I've had my eye trained on him for nearly a year now.

"While he was noticing you," he asks me, "did *you* notice anything about him? Was he waiting for anyone? Watching for anything?"

I tell him that he didn't appear to be waiting or watching. That he made no phone calls, was fairly intent on eating and did, indeed, flirt with my mother. This last bit Drew takes with a grain of salt, which was the way it was intended.

"And he had a short conversation with Mario," I tell him. "I think he might have been unhappy with the food, though he didn't send it back."

Drew asks what makes me think he was dissatisfied, and I tell him that the discussion seemed acrimonious and that Mario looked distressed when he left the table. Drew makes a note and says he'll look into it and asks about anyone else in the restaurant. Did I see anyone who didn't seem to belong, anyone who was watching the victim, anyone looking suspicious?

"Besides my mother?" I ask him, and Mom huffs and blows her cigarette smoke in my direction.

I tell him that there were several deliveries, the kitchen staff going in and out the back door to grab a smoke. He stops me and asks what I was doing checking out the back door of the restaurant.

Proudly—because, while he was off forgetting me, dropping by only once in a while to say hi to Jesse, my son, or drop something by for one of my daughters that he thought they might like, I was getting on with my life—I tell him that I'm decorating the place.

He looks genuinely impressed. "Commercial customers? That's great," he says. Okay, that's what he *ought* to say. What he actually says is "Whatever pays the bills."

"Howard Rosen, the famous restaurant critic, got her the job," my mother says. "You met him—the good-looking, distinguished gentleman with the *real* job, something to be proud of. I guess you've never read his reviews in *Newsday*."

Drew, without missing a beat, tells her that Howard's reviews are on the top of his list, as soon as he learns how to read.

"I only meant—" my mother starts, but both of us assure her that we know just what she meant.

"So," Drew says. "Deliveries?"

I tell him that Mario would know better than I, but that I saw vegetables come in, maybe fish and linens.

"This is the second restaurant job Howard's got her," my mother tells Drew.

"At least she's getting *something* out of the relationship," he says.

"If he were here," my mother says, ignoring the insinuation, "he'd be comforting her instead of interrogating her. He'd be making sure we're both all right after such an ordeal."

"I'm sure he would," Drew agrees, then looks me in the eyes as if he's measuring my tolerance for shock. Quietly he adds, "But then maybe he doesn't know just what strong stuff your daughter's made of."

It's the closest thing to a tender moment I can expect from Drew Scoones. My mother breaks the spell. "She gets that from me," she says.

Both Drew and I take a minute, probably to pray that's all I inherited from her.

"I'm just trying to save you some time and effort," my mother tells him. "My money's on Howard."

Drew withers her with a look and mutters something that sounds suspiciously like "fool's gold." Then he excuses himself to go back to work.

I catch his sleeve and ask if it's all right for us to leave. He says sure, he knows where we live. I say goodbye to Mario. I assure him that I will have some sketches for him in a few days, all the while hoping that this murder doesn't cancel his redecorating plans. I need the money desperately, the alternative being borrowing from my parents and being strangled by the strings.

My mother is strangely quiet all the way to her house. She doesn't tell me what a loser Drew Scoones is—despite his good looks—and how I was obviously drooling over him. She doesn't ask me where Howard is taking me tonight or warn me not to tell my father about what happened because he will worry about us both and no doubt insist we see our respective psychiatrists.

She fidgets nervously, opening and closing her purse over and over again.

"You okay?" I ask her. After all, she's just found a dead man on the toilet... and tough as she is that's got to be upsetting.

When she doesn't answer me I pull over to the side of the road.

"Mom?" She refuses to meet my eyes. "You want me to take you to see Dr. Cohen?"

She looks out the window as if she's just realized we're on Broadway in Woodmere. "Aren't we near Marvin's Jewelers?" she asks, pulling something out of her purse.

"What have you got, Mother?" I ask, prying open her fingers to find the murdered man's ring.

"It was on the sink," she says in answer to my dropped jaw. "I was going to get his name and address and have you return it to him so that he could ask you out. I thought it was a sign that the two of you were meant to be together."

"He's dead, Mom. You understand that, right?" I ask. You never can tell when my mother is fine and when she's in la-la land.

"Well, I didn't know that," she shouts at me. "Not at the time."

I ask why she didn't give it to Drew, realize that she wouldn't give Drew the time in a clock shop and add, "...or one of the other policemen?"

"For heaven's sake," she tells me. "The man is dead, Teddi, and I took his ring. How would that look?"

Before I can tell her it looks just the way it is, she pulls out a cigarette and threatens to light it.

"I mean, really," she says, shaking her head like it's my brains that are loose. "What does he need with it now?"

nocturne™

WAS HE HER SAVIOR
OR HER NIGHTMARE?

HAUNTED
LISA CHILDS

Years ago, Ariel and her sisters were separated for
their own protection. Now the man who vowed
revenge on her family has resumed the hunt, and
Ariel must warn her sisters before it's too late.
The closer she comes to finding them, the more
secretive her fiancé becomes. Can she trust the man
she plans to spend eternity with? Or has he been
waiting for the perfect moment to destroy her?

On sale December 2006.

SNHDEC

In February, expect *MORE* from

as it increases to six titles per month.

What's to come...

Rancher and Protector

Part of the

Western Weddings

miniseries

BY JUDY CHRISTENBERRY

The Boss's Pregnancy Proposal

BY RAYE MORGAN

Don't miss February's
incredible line up of authors!

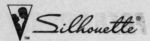